JOEY
LEONARD'S
LAST
HORROR MOVIE
MARATHON

ALSO BY KEVIN LUCIA

Things Slip Through
Devourer of Souls
Through A Mirror, Darkly
A Night at Old Webb
Things You Need
Mystery Road
October Nights
The Night Road
Drowning

FORTHCOMING
When the Lights Go Out
The Horror at Pleasant Brook
We All Go Into the Dark

JOEY LEONARD'S LAST HORROR MOVIE MARATHON

KEVIN LUCIA

BLEEDING
EDGE BOOKS

ISBN: 979-8-218-13334-4
Cover artwork by Ben Baldwin
Book design & formatting by Todd Keisling | Dullington Design Co.

Bleeding Edge Books
www.bleedingedgepub.com

To all of us who thrived during the age of Be Kind, Rewind.

"We live on a placid island of ignorance in the midst of black seas of infinity, and it was not meant that we should voyage far."

— *H. P. Lovecraft*

1

Showbiz Video
Henry Street
Clifton Heights, New York
9:00 PM

"**D**id you know Brad Pitt auditioned for Michael in *Phantasm II*? It would've been his first major role."

"Really?" Deputy Tony Phelps, in plainclothes, with his badge clipped to his belt, wore a black and red checkered flannel over a white t-shirt and jeans. Even without the badge on his belt, however, you could tell he was a cop. Something about the way he stood. The way he carried himself. Luckily, he was one of the good ones. "You know how many times I've watched the Phantasm movies and never knew that?"

Joey nodded as he knelt on the floor next to a huge plastic bin, removing VHS cases from the "Comedy" section and gently, almost reverently, securing them inside. "Yep.

He auditioned for the part, but Don Coscarelli passed on him. Didn't have the 'look' he wanted for Michael."

"I did *not* know that."

"Yeah. Thing is, though," Joey took *Roxanne, Superbad,* and *Stepbrothers* off the rack and gently packed them, "lots of folks wonder if Coscarelli was being difficult because he'd never wanted to recast Michael in the first place. He was forced to by Universal Pictures when they picked up the second film, which offered a bigger budget and wider distribution… at the expense of A. Michael Baldwin, whom Universal didn't think looked 'cinematic' enough. Whatever the hell *that* means."

Joey looked up at Tony. "Fans were *not* happy."

"I bet. Always wondered why they recast Michael for only one movie." Tony shook his head. "Funny thing is, I don't even remember who played Michael in *II.* Must've not done much after."

"James Lebros," Joey said as he resumed pulling VHS and DVD cases off the rack and storing them in the bin, "and he actually did well for himself. Acted in lots of movies. Was in the original *Point Break*, and its remake. Was also in 1998's remake of *Psycho.* Still acting, actually."

"Huh."

Joey paused in his sorting and said wistfully, "Y'know, *Phantasm II* has to be one of my favorite movies of all time. There's something… simple, about it. Something pure.

It's Reggie and Mike, cruising a wasted countryside in the 'Cuda, hunting the Tall Man, and killing monsters. That's it; that's all."

Tony smiled. "Sounds like the perfect world for a horror fan."

Joey smiled in return. "Sure does." He resumed sorting movies into the gray tote before him.

"Damn, Joey. You never cease to amaze me. All this movie shit you know."

"Yup," Joey said, "that's me. A vast repository of pointless movie trivia."

"*Not* pointless. You should write a book about this stuff."

Joey's shrug felt limp because, of course, he'd thought about doing exactly that so many times. Especially with the recent boom in self-publishing. Problem was, all the things he knew - hundreds of random, assorted facts of horror cinema - weren't that special. Any cinephile with a computer already blogged about those things every single day.

"Nah. Lots of people know the same stuff I do. I'm not unique, honestly."

He could always write such a book for himself. But for some reason, that felt hollow. Empty.

Just like his store soon would be.

Joey grabbed the last DVDs and VHS cases off the comedy racks and packed them neatly into the gray bin.

He gave the bin's contents a last once-over to make sure everything was packed together snuggly, nodded once, then closed the bin's covers. They clicked shut with a terribly final sound.

Joey stood, brushed his hands off, and looked at the bare shelves, racks, and displays of Showbiz Video. *Formerly* Showbiz Video, of course. Who knew what would take its place? Maybe it would become a kitschy novelty store selling cheap Adirondack tourist merchandise, sweaters and t-shirts, and probably, ironically, self-published trail guides.

For now, Showbiz Video was a blank space. All the VHS tapes and DVDs lovingly packed away in gray bins like the one sitting at his feet. Movie posters taken down, carefully rolled up and secured with rubber bands and returned to their original shipping tubes, which he'd kept over the years. Cardboard displays, which he'd stored carefully since becoming store manager, had been raffled off to customers, with the proceeds going to Bassler Memorial Library. With the exception of the shelves and racks, nothing remained to hint at what had once been Clifton Heights' only video rental store. The last video rental store in all of Webb County, and even Adirondack Park.

Showbiz Video. His home and his life, for the past twenty years, now empty and bereft of meaning.

Just like him.

"You okay?"

Joey looked at Tony and smiled sheepishly, doing his best to hide the dull ache of despair pulsing in his gut. He shrugged, looking back at his newly empty store. "As okay as I can be, I guess. I mean… we knew this was coming. The writing's been on the wall for *years* now."

He faced Tony and offered him a rueful grin. "Twenty years ago, when I was first hired, Showbiz thought maybe they'd be closed in five years. The Blockbuster in Utica kept calling, offering to buy us out. People were peer-sharing movies online, and DVDs had already started replacing VHS. If we hadn't started offering DVDs to rent alongside VHS, we might've closed."

"But you survived," Tony said with a grin.

Joey shrugged again. "Sure we did. Thanks to lots of older folks in Clifton Heights who didn't want to switch to DVDs and who were scared of the internet. That, and our owner - Old Man Kretzmer - didn't worry too much about making a profit. So long as we broke even, the rent was paid and the electricity stayed on, he was content to let us go about our business."

Joey snorted and shook his head. "That, and I think the old buzzard loved telling the Utica Blockbuster where they could stick their buy-out offer every time they called. Cantankerous old fart."

Tony chuckled. "That's a fact. And hey, you guys got

the last laugh. Utica Blockbuster closed eleven years ago, while you guys kept going."

"Yeah, but only because Kretzmer was so lenient. Sales dropped a lot when Netflix started streaming in '07. When Roku got big? Along with streaming on phones, and all these apps?" Joey waved dismissively. "I'm surprised we made it this long."

"You would've made it longer," Tony said softly, "if Old Man Kretzmer hadn't passed away last month."

"I guess. I think he was considering closing before that, though. He hadn't authorized any inventory purchases for almost six months, which wasn't normal." He offered Tony a regretful smile. "Even if he was still alive, I think he still might've closed us, eventually."

He bent over, grabbed the bin's handholds, and hoisted it onto the long and now bare sales counter next to other bins. "At least most of the movies went to new homes in the fire sale. The rest," he said as he began a last inspection of each bin, flipping open their lids and checking to see everything was neatly packed, "are going to the library, to expand their video section." He flipped the comedy bin closed and moved to the next bin, which was the first of three science fiction/fantasy bins.

"What about the horror movies?" Tony asked in a knowing tone.

Joey checked the sci/fi/fantasy bin, closed it, and moved

to the next one. He grinned over his shoulder at Tony. "Old Man Kretzmer willed those to me, of course, to become part of my already exhaustive personal collection."

Tony smiled, having watched movies at Joey's house often. "I know. I've seen it firsthand. But don't you already own half of these movies?"

Joey finished a quick examination of the second sci/fi/fantasy bin and moved to the third. "Yeah, but some of them I only have on DVD. Having the VHS versions will add a nice touch of nostalgia. And anything I don't want, I'll donate to Handy's Pawn and Thrift, because the library didn't want the horror movies."

Joey closed the bin's lid and moved to the next one. Both he and Tony fell silent for several minutes as he sorted through the DVDs and tapes, making sure they were packed well.

Tony finally said in a somber voice, "What are you going to do next?"

Joey stopped for a moment, hands lying on the packed DVDs and VHS cases. He breathed deeply, closed the bin's covers, then turned and faced Tony. He tried not to let his friend's worried expression depress him, and he only partially succeeded.

He folded his arms and again looked around the empty racks and shelves. "Well, as I said. The writing's been on the wall for a while. About ten years ago I doubled the amount going from my paycheck to my 401k. Also started saving extra wherever I could." He shrugged, feeling a strange weakness in his gut. "And, y'know. After Beth called things off a few years ago? Well."

He looked back at Tony and smiled weakly. "I never spent any of the money I saved for the wedding and the new house. Just squirreled it away and started adding to it."

He shrugged again, hating the fact that it was all he did lately. "I've got enough saved up to last a while. Plus, Kretzmer left me a nice severance in his will. The wolves won't be howling at my door for a bit."

Tony gave him a penetrating look, eyes narrowed, as if he sensed Joey wasn't being completely honest with him. "I'm not talking about money, y'know."

Joey nodded, and only said, "I'll figure it out. Always do."

Tony said nothing right away. Just looked at him intently, as if he could divine the answers he sought simply by staring at Joey. After a few more minutes, however, he relented with a sigh. "Okay. But remember - we've been friends since junior high. You're not alone. You know that, right?"

Joey licked his lips, swallowed, and then lied. "Yeah. I know."

Tony didn't look convinced. "Reach out, man. If you need anything." He nodded toward his car parked outside. "I've got the overnight shift all weekend on patrol. See you Monday night for a few beers at The Inn?"

"Sure," Joey lied again as he returned to checking the bins, "you can count on it."

2

Forty-five minutes after Tony Phelps left, Joey had the store ready to close for the last time. All the bins with their assorted DVDs and VHS tapes - organized by genre - he'd stacked next to the front door for easy access tomorrow morning. Earl Flannigan from the library was coming at nine for them. Once that was done, Joey would visit the law offices of Spellman & O'Hara on Main Street who were handling Old Man Kretzmer's Affairs. After that last meeting, it would close the book on Showbiz Video for good.

It had taken Joey far too long to clean his office out back. As soon as Tony Phelps left, Joey walked slowly past the bare sales counter, out back, every step dragging, his feet feeling encased in lead. At his office door, he reached inside and flipped on the light. As he entered, he felt a heavy weight descend upon his heart.

An empty cardboard box sat next to the dingy metal desk against the far wall. He sat in the battered but still-comfortable rolling chair with the intention of emptying the contents of the desk into the box, after which he'd carefully take down his personal movie posters from the walls. Instead, he just sat there, soaking up the office for the last time.

Once, it had been nothing more than a storage area for mops, buckets, brooms, and the cardboard movie displays the former manager never bothered to put in the store. Twenty years ago, Stu Owen ran Showbiz Video with the efficient yet apathetic air of a man who was simply waiting for the next dead-end job to come along. A retired engineer, Stu had only been running the store for five years when Joey came on, but every day he performed his duties as if he was on the tail-end of a thirty-year career at the lumbermill. He moved and thought slowly and exerted only minimal effort when engaging with his customers and employees.

Stu kept the books balanced and the cash register even at the end of every shift. He made sure the store was adequately staffed at all times, and that the store's paperwork (sent to Old Man Kretzmer quarterly) was always in order. That, however, was the extent of Stu's investment in Showbiz. He cared as little for movies as he'd cared for books when he'd worked part-time as a clerk at the library, and as little for whatever post-retirement job he moved on to next.

Joey worked under Stu's listless leadership for three years before Stu accepted a position as the night shift manager at the twenty-four-hour Mobilmart on Haverton Road. During that period Stu became more and more content to allow Joey additional responsibilities at Showbiz like calling overdue rentals, purchasing new stock, and balancing the books each month. For Stu, it was a win–win scenario: pulling down manager pay and benefits, while farming most of his work onto a recent college graduate who was eager to make his bones and perfectly happy to work sixty hours a week.

For Joey, it presented an excellent opportunity to gain the skills he'd need to someday take over the store. He knew Old Man Kretzmer hired from within, and not only did Joey sense Stu wasn't long in leaving, he knew his co-workers, two seniors at Clifton Heights High and a college student taking a "break" which had lasted three years, had no interest in running the store when Stu inevitably and numbly did move on. Joey had every intention of making himself the prime candidate for the manager's position when it became available.

He'd known exactly what to change. He'd put up all the movie displays Stu just tossed in the storeroom, added to the store's inventory from local indie filmmakers, hosted premier parties for new releases, and teamed up with Earl Flannigan for the annual "Fright-Fest" movie marathon held at Raedeker Park. There was more, too. He only needed to be patient and use Stu's remaining days to develop the skills he needed.

He'd shown patience and developed those skills. Stu moved on, and Kretzmer (by proxy, of course, through his lawyer), hired Joey as store manager. All the plans he'd carefully constructed came true, even teaming up with Earl for the Fright-Fest. He did all those things and more, for the next twenty years.

Until now.

Joey spun slowly in his chair. His gaze passed from the *Phantasm* poster over his desk to his left, traveling over the *Evil Dead* posters - *Evil Dead 1 & 2, Armies of Darkness* - then *Real Genius, Caddyshack,* and all the way around the room to the *Star Wars* posters, *Heat,* and *Ghost and the Darkness* (his favorite Val Kilmer movie). He'd never meant to spend twenty years here, of course. Initially he'd looked at it as nothing more than a good resume-builder as he applied to film schools in New York and California. He could pay off some bills and gain front-line experience with distribution companies. But as the years passed, his film school applications were rejected via professional, respectful, concise letters, and his tenure as manager of Showbiz Video stretched further and further into the foreseeable future.

He could've easily grown bitter and disillusioned,

becoming every bit as numb as Stu Owens was. A curious thing happened, however. The young man once eager to leave and make his mark in the film industry found himself happy right where he was, in his childhood home.

Even so, while his determination to find his place in the movie business had faded, his love of cinema continued to blossom as he realized Showbiz Video provided everything he needed. Beth had ultimately disagreed and Joey realized when they finally parted ways, he wasn't all that sad. He still had the video store, after all, and his place in Clifton Heights society. His role in Clifton Heights, his *purpose.*

Except that was gone now, too.

A profound sense of grief filled Joey, weighing his heart down even worse. Deep inside, he'd always known Showbiz Video wouldn't last forever. It always had an expiration date, and even though they'd staved it off as long as possible, there was never any preventing it. He'd been deceiving himself, and even worse: he'd known it. In his heart, he'd known it and had refused to admit it to himself.

Beth had known it, too.

"*I don't understand,*" Beth's ghost-voice whispered, "*I've tried, but I don't. You've been invited to teach film at the high school and the community college. Jobs with benefits and tenure. You don't need this store anymore.*"

He'd considered both those positions but had dismissed them immediately. He just didn't want to teach. He also didn't want to work for someone else or deal with high school and college students who'd see his class as an easy 'A' and nothing more. The only teachers he knew who were happy were the ones who'd retired early and were now doing what *they* wanted. Not exactly shining examples of vocational bliss. He didn't see the point of taking a job he was going to get sick of and quit, and he'd told Beth so.

That, of course, had been the beginning of the end for them. She said she still cared for him, maybe even loved him, but seeing as how he didn't care enough about their future to do the responsible thing, she didn't see any reason for them to continue. He could've argued with her on a number of points, of course. He could have told her it was more responsible for him to hold onto a job he loved (even though its future appeared dim) than take a job he'd probably hate, that such a situation would make him miserable to her and everyone around him.

But he knew there wasn't any convincing Beth when her mind was made up. Also, it wasn't worth the angst and prolonged separation. And that was how they'd ended things. Amicably, and as numbly as Stu Owen lived his life.

In his darker moments, Joey often wished their breakup had been cataclysmic, or at least more dramatic. As it was, it passed by like his film school rejections, and she was in his rearview mirror before he knew it.

Joey pushed down these thoughts as he always did

when they reared their ugly heads, but it was more difficult than usual this time. The future stretched out before him, a gray, empty highway with no end. He'd been lying to Tony, of course, when he claimed he'd "figure it out like always." He had no idea what to do or how to figure it out, and if he didn't find something to occupy his time right away, if he didn't find something *else* to focus on…

Joey sighed once more and shoved those thoughts away with even more difficulty. He spun on the chair toward the desk, opened a drawer, and began emptying its contents into the cardboard box next to his feet, trying to fill his mind with white noise, and only partially succeeding.

3

An hour later, Joey was reclining on his sofa, wearing only a t-shirt and shorts, in the basement den of his small Concord home. He'd purchased it not long after securing the manager's position at Showbiz. It had also been right around the time his application rejections had started rolling in, when he'd realized, even if only subconsciously, he'd be staying in Clifton Heights a lot longer than he'd initially intended. When it became even clearer he wasn't heading off to graduate school anytime soon, he saved up the money, and about two years after buying the house, remodeled its basement into a home theater.

He'd started collecting movies in earnest around then. Today, the fruits of his labors lined the walls of his den, stored in simple but skillfully built wooden shelves which reached from floor to ceiling. He collected one genre in particular: horror.

It didn't matter what kind. He loved them all, from ghost stories, cosmic horror, body horror and slasher films, classic black and white films by Val Lewiston, independent "arthouse horror" (even A24 films), psychological horror, cheezy low-budget eighties horror, to big budget blockbusters. It didn't matter. He even owned a small collection of Italian Giallo films, though admittedly only a half-dozen - Fulci movies in particular – had ever caught his fancy.

He'd sheet-rocked the walls and paneled them when he'd remodeled the basement. He'd also sheet-rocked and stuccoed the ceiling and installed recessed lighting. For some reason, however, he'd never carpeted the concrete floor. Instead, he'd painted it glossy black and bought several large horror-themed rugs (like the huge Universal Monsters rug at the foot of the sofa). The glossy black floors set off the rugs nicely.

In front of the sofa, of course, Joey's fifty-inch flat screen Samsung television hung from the wall, mounted over a smaller shelf filled with horror movies. Also, though Joey subscribed to almost every good streaming horror movie app that existed, he preferred his physical media collection, so his Smart TV was rigged up to both a DVD/

Blu-Ray player and a VCR. Both players sat on a small, sturdy shelf mounted on the wall next to the flatscreen.

He'd spent countless hours down here watching movies, both alone and occasionally with Tony Phelps and a few others – but increasingly alone, as of late. He had also enjoyed many date nights down here with Beth, which, of course, had often led to *other* activities he didn't want to think about at all, so he quickly shut the door on those memories.

His favorite activity in the movie den was his monthly Horror Movie Marathon. After closing the store on a Friday night, Joey took the weekend off – from work, socializing, even Beth – and spent it in his den, watching horror movies and drinking. The week before his marathon, he made a careful perusal of his collection, getting a feel for the movies he wanted to watch that weekend. He chose whatever called to him, with no predetermined selections in mind.

This whole week, however, nothing had called to him. He hadn't searched his shelves either, giving no thought as to what he might watch. And now here he sat, an hour after coming home from Showbiz Video for the last time, staring at the black flat-screen with a glass of Tullamore Dew Irish whiskey (neat, about three fingers) in his hand and the bins of horror movies Old Man Kretzmer had willed him from the store sitting at his feet.

Of course, he had a drink in his hand. His second, in fact. That was a given, anymore. It was an aspect of his monthly movie marathon which had grown in importance over the years. At first it had only been a few beers, because what was the point of getting so smashed you couldn't even remember the movies you watched, much less stay awake all the way through them?

However, as time passed, he drank more and more during his marathons. At first, he chalked it up as increasing tolerance. He couldn't deny that he had a harder time remembering what movies he'd watched, nor could he deny the worsening hangovers he experienced Saturday and Sunday mornings.

Of course, he tried telling himself it had just been a tough work-week, or he'd felt under the weather and had a slight cold, or he wasn't a kid anymore, what could he expect?

In all his rationalizing, he never once attributed it to too much drinking. He'd kept his increasing alcohol consumption firmly in denial, ignoring the multiplying beer bottles in the returnables bin and the whiskey bottles in the recyclables bin.

He didn't ask himself *why* he was drinking more and didn't worry about it. He didn't question it, or probe his psyche for reasons. If he was self-medicating, he didn't want to know the cause, he just wanted to *medicate* and leave it at that.

Spurred on by these thoughts, Joey took a healthy swallow of his whiskey. The liquor burned gently down his throat, settling into a warm glow in his belly. Maybe he wouldn't do a movie marathon this weekend. Maybe he'd just sit here and methodically drink until he had the courage to...

His smartphone rang, playing the *Halloween* movie theme. He regularly cycled through his favorite horror movie theme songs as ringtones. He picked it up and frowned, then frowned even deeper when he saw who was calling.

Beth.

Of course it was. He was hardly surprised. Tonight, Showbiz Video closed its doors for good. Coincidentally- or not- its end had fallen on the weekend of his movie marathon. She also knew he'd be drinking (an issue she'd become increasingly concerned about when they were still engaged, but which she'd never addressed openly). So, of course she'd worry, and of course she'd call.

His thumb hovered over the 'reject call' icon.

But why not talk to her? All she'd do was ask him if he was okay, or reassure him she still cared. He knew this, of course, and it didn't make things easier. Then she would gently probe his emotional state. She wouldn't lecture him or berate him. It wasn't her style.

"What the fuck. Why not?"

He thumbed the green "accept" icon and put the phone to his ear. "Hey, you."

"*Hey yourself.*" A pause, and then in true Beth fashion, she came gently to the point. "*Just wanted to know how you're doing.*"

Joey smiled. One of the things he'd always appreciated about Beth was her forthrightness. Ironically, it was also one of the things which had annoyed him, too. "I'm fine. Why wouldn't I be?" He said it coyly, of course. With a slight tease in his tone which he knew infuriated her in that pleasing sort of way lovers often feel for each other. The memory of it felt good, but it hurt, too.

Beth snorted. He imagined her annoyed smile, and that only made him feel more happy/sad. "*You know what I'm talking about. The store, dumbass.*"

Part of him wanted to laugh. *Dumbass* had been her pet name for him, and its use had never failed to earn a chuckle, or at least a grin. Now, however, all he felt was a dull emptiness. He blew out a breath and said, "Oh. That."

"*Joey, I'm so sorry. I know how much that store meant to you.*" The kicker? Beth *was* sorry, and she *did* know how much it had meant to him. Her advice to leave the store for another career hadn't ever been malicious or demeaning. She'd just wanted the best for him and their future, their best *practical* future. He couldn't fault her for that at all.

And Joey found he could be more truthful with her

than he could with Tony. "Thanks. I mean, it wasn't a big shock. We've known for a few months. Ever since Kretzmer kicked, so we've had time to prepare. It hasn't been emotionally jarring, at least."

"*But?*"

He shook his head. Damn, was she able to see right through him. Able to call him on his bullshit, without sounding pesky or invasive. "Well, obviously I'm not *happy* about it. And I... well, to be honest?"

"*Yes.*   *Please.*"

He took a deep breath, then plunged forward. "What the hell am I going to do now? Work at the gas station? The library? Do what every other unemployed guy does in this town and work at the lumbermill? Think I'd rather shoot myself right in the face."

"*Hey.*" Beth's tone quickly grew stern. "*Not cool.*"

"Okay, relax. You know how I feel about guns. If I was gonna go, it wouldn't be that way."

"*See, when you say stuff like that, it worries me. You've always had a morbid streak, y'know.*"

He certainly couldn't argue with her on that point. Joey had often wondered if that's where his love of horror stemmed from, if horror had become his vicarious and safe way of confronting death over and over. He and Beth had talked about that a lot. It was one of the things he missed most from their relationship.

"I guess so. But a morbid streak doesn't mean suicidal."

At least, not always.

"*I know. Normally, I'd never think that you'd...*" A pause, and then, "*but I've been worried about you all week. With the store closing, this weekend being your marathon... plus, I knew you'd be drinking.*"

That was all she'd say. She wouldn't nag or lecture, just state her case, and move on. She put things out in the open but didn't belabor them. She let them speak for themselves. He glanced at the drink in his hand, knowing that after they hung up, he'd slug the drink right back and pour himself a third. Maybe four fingers, this time. "I'll be fine. I'm probably only gonna watch a few movies, go to bed before midnight. Not even in the mood to drink, really."

liar, liar

pants on fire

"*I'm sure,*" Beth said, her tone indicating she didn't believe him, but she wasn't going to press her case, either. Joey often wondered if things would have turned out differently between them if they'd been more honest and direct with each other. Maybe if either of them had just said plainly what they thought, things would've ended much sooner, or maybe they would've even resolved their differences and come to a compromise. As it was, they'd danced around each other passively for almost five years, and here they were.

"Just don't drink until you pass out, okay? You always feel awful the day after."

Even though she wasn't there to see it, Joey lifted his whiskey in mock-salute. "Aye aye, cap'n."

Beth snorted, as she always did when he'd responded as thus. *"Dumbass."* A pause, and then, *"All right. I'm off to bed. I know you won't, but I'm going to offer anyway. Call me if you need anything. Okay?"*

This time he didn't have the heart to make light. He responded simply with, "Will do."

"Have a good night, Joey. Or at least, a tolerable one."

"You too." Having nothing more to say, Joey hung up, but not before hearing Beth hang up first. He set the phone down on the lampstand next to the futon and took another swig of whiskey. It was a smaller one, perhaps tempered by Beth's concern. He sat up with a grunt and stared at the gray tote full of the horror movies Old Man Kretzmer had willed him from Showbiz Video, suddenly thinking about the odd way Kretzmer's lawyers had handled the whole thing. Instead of simply letting him take the horror movies he wanted directly from the shelves, they'd insisted on collecting the movies themselves, itemizing them, and then recording them as "gifted" to Joey. For "tax reasons," apparently. That didn't make much sense, but Joey hadn't felt like questioning them, so he didn't.

True to the lawyer's words, all of Showbiz Video's

horror movies were collected by moving men hired by Kretzmer's lawyers and carted away in the same tote now sitting at Joey's feet. Two days ago, the tote was delivered to him with an itemized list of all the movies inside. Oddly enough, he hadn't bothered to look the movies over, or peruse the list. He'd told himself it was because he already knew which movies the tote contained, having been the store manager for the past twenty years. He'd been lying to himself, however. He knew it.

The *real* reason why he hadn't opened the tote yet was because it would be admitting it was over. As much as he wanted both Tony and Beth to believe he could handle it, he knew the God's honest truth: He couldn't handle it. Wasn't handling it at *all*.

He sat and stared at the gray tote, raised his glass, and drained the whiskey from it. As he felt the liquor blaze a glowing trail of warmth to his belly, he set the glass on the lampstand next to his phone. At last, he reached out, flipped the tote's lids open, and started searching for a movie to watch.

4

After twenty minutes of rifling through several DVDs and VHS tapes, Joey finally settled on a horror-comedy. *The Stuff*, a movie about alien goo masquerading as highly addictive ice cream which took over people's minds. Despite its cheesiness, the movie held up better than Joey had expected, also offering much more of a social commentary on the rampant commercialism of the eighties than he remembered the first time he'd watched it.

Regardless, its tongue-in-cheek nature was the perfect movie for Joey's current mood, which still weighed heavy on his heart. In fact, he found himself enjoying the movie so much, he only downed one drink the entire movie, and only two fingers of whiskey at that.

His mood improved considerably, Joey felt himself getting into the movie marathon spirit. Rummaging through the tote again, he decided on the ultra-low-budget yet oddly charming *Night Vision*, starring absolutely nobody. He'd seen the movie as a kid on some late-night cable access channel and had loved it, so it was one of his first official store purchases when he became manager at Showbiz. He'd had to resort to eBay for the only copy he could find. It cost thirty bucks because it was so far off market no one distributed it anymore, and at the time, no one was selling it on Amazon. These days it was streaming free on several platforms, but twenty years ago, it was hidden in the dim reaches of VHS movie past.

In some ways, of course, it made a maudlin sort of sense. He was grieving the loss of Showbiz by watching the first movie he'd purchased as manager.

Fortunately, once he popped *Night Vision* into the VCR and started watching it, he was able to dismiss such gray thoughts (another glass of whiskey helped greatly), and enjoy one of the most ridiculous movies he'd ever seen. It was about a desperate writer moving to the big city to find his inspiration and fortune, and the demonically-possessed VCR that helps him achieve his wildest writing dreams… at the cost of his soul. His earlier temperance forgotten, Joey enjoyed *several* glasses of whiskey throughout the movie. By its end, he had a more-than-adequate buzz going. He felt coated in a pleasantly warm fog which insulated him from all of life's cares.

"Seems like a good place to stop for a bit," Joey muttered

as he leaned forward unsteadily and ejected the VHS tape. He replaced it in its sleeve and set it aside. "A good place to stop, indeed."

He belched, long and deep. His nose stung with the whiskey's afterburn.

He felt as if he was floating over the gray tote, searching for another movie. He knew deep down there'd be no stopping tonight. Usually, by the time he was telling himself it was "time to stop" he'd already passed the point of no return.

He wasn't consciously thinking this as he searched for another movie, of course. He was thinking maybe he'd watch something trippy next. Maybe *Demon Wind* or *Highway to Hell*. It was always fun to watch such films when he'd had "a little" to drink. What he pulled out of the tote, however, wasn't a weird, trippy, campy film. It was a store-bought VHS tape. The sleeve said *Memorex*. Nothing was written on the sleeve's label.

Joey frowned and flipped it over so he could see the label on the spine. Only one thing was written on it. *Numero Vitae*.

Joey stared at the label, mind working sluggishly against all the booze he'd consumed. Even though the phrase sounded Latin, he felt fairly confident he knew what the words meant. *Numero* was probably "number." And *vitae* he *thought* meant being or existence. Number being? Number existence?

He leaned sideways and clumsily grabbed his smartphone off the lampstand at the end of the sofa. He swiped his thumb across it to unlock it, then tapped the Google icon. And because he'd had "a little" to drink and didn't feel like fumbling with his fat fingers, he tapped the microphone in the search bar, held the phone up to his mouth and said, "Translate: Numero vitae."

The phone *binged*, and he looked at the results. First and foremost was the Google Translate definition: Numbers of Life.

"What the fuck does that mean?" He glanced at the tape again, wondering just what the hell it was, and how it had ended up in the tote of movies from Kretzmer's lawyers. It certainly wasn't a tape from Showbiz Video, *that* was for sure.

The thought occurred to Joey it must've belonged to Old Man Kretzmer himself. Someone had screwed up sorting through his things, and somehow the tape had ended up in *his* tote. Another thought occurred to him, this one uniquely terrifying in its own way. Maybe the tape contained footage of... a personal and *intimate* nature.

The whiskey in Joey's belly soured at the thought of watching some kinky homemade porn Kretzmer had made, even though *Numero Vitae* or *Numbers of Life* was an odd way to label a sex-tape. Of course, one of his college buddies labeled his bootleg porn as "nature videos," "National Geographic Special," and "Good Fishing," so…

He hefted the tape experimentally, which, he immediately realized, was stupid. As if a homemade sex-tape weighed more, or something. He stared at the tape for a few minutes longer, whispered "Numero Vitae" to himself a few times, then said, "Why the hell not?"

He leaned forward. Popped the video into the VCR, and pressed PLAY. He settled back onto the couch, took a healthy swig of whiskey, and watched as the static on the screen resolved into an image.

At first, Joey had a hard time distinguishing shapes and making sense of what he saw. Everything was dark shadows and gradations of gray. Eventually, however — maybe because the picture quality improved and sharpened, maybe because he was focusing harder, or maybe simply because his eyes became adjusted to the dim image — he was able to make out the corners of a dark room. Mostly unfurnished, except for…

He leaned forward. In the center of the screen stood four metal poles, arranged in a square. Hanging from them, facing into the enclosed square were black rectangles. They appeared familiar, but he couldn't say why.

Also, the angle of the video suggested a camera mounted high on the wall, looking down on the square space inside the four poles. The view offered a more three-dimensional perspective of the space inside the poles, and Joey thought that was to provide a more detailed view of what might happen there…

Why'd he have that thought? What could possibly happen? He was instinctively viewing the space as a holding area of sorts, almost like… a *cage*. That didn't make sense either. There were only four poles, without fencing or anything else to keep anything inside, *if* the poles were meant to keep anything inside at all. Maybe the poles were… electrified, somehow? Maybe they emitted some sort of electrical current or field which could hold something inside, but that was nonsensical.

An odd (almost ridiculous in its melodrama) thought occurred to him in such cold clarity he shivered. He should stop the movie. Pop the VHS tape out, crack the case open, and rip the film inside to shreds. Nothing good would come from him watching any more of what was on that tape.

Which, of course, was one of the worst meta, postmodern horror clichés ever.

"Fuck it," he whispered, and let the tape run. He shifted on the sofa, thinking maybe that was it. Maybe it was a low-budget attempt at meta-found-footage horror. But why record it on a VHS tape with outdated equipment? A tape that appeared over twenty-years old. The first found footage movie — before *The Blair Witch* or even

The Last Broadcast — was *The McPherson Tapes*, a mostly anticlimactic and dull home-movie account of an alien invasion in the middle of a birthday party. It had been obscure until streaming devices started bringing obscure movies out of the past (as with *Night Vision*). Was this something similar to that? But what was it doing in the videos from Showbiz? *He'd* certainly never ordered it. Had never even seen it, for sure.

Something moved near the bottom of the screen. A dark shape, which appeared circular, almost like…

Joey leaned forward further, almost losing his balance, even though he felt abruptly sober. It was a head. Someone's head, and if he looked even closer, he could almost make out the large headphones they were wearing.

As if sensing his shift in focus (and that had to be a coincidence), the camera's focus shifted slightly, panning downward. The strange four poles and its enclosed square remained on screen, but now Joey could clearly see the back of the head and shoulders of a stout man sitting at a small, square table. The figure indeed wore headphones. Standing next to him was an old VHS camera on a tripod, aimed at the square inside the four poles.

For some reason, Joey no longer thought this was a badly-made mockumentary. This was… real, somehow. No credits, no title screen, no character dialogue or sound effects. Just a small, dark and unfurnished room with four poles with boxes mounted on them and a man sitting in a chair facing the square space inside the four poles, being recorded as *he* recorded whatever was supposed to be happening inside those poles.

A screech exploded from the flatscreen. Joey lurched back, because the noise had *substance*. Like it was *reaching* out to strike him. He groped for the remote lying next to him on the sofa. Suddenly feeling much clearer as a jolt of adrenaline flushed through him. The wailing sound waxed and waned, hurting his ears, pounding in his head. By the time he found the remote and pointed it at the TV, however, the screeching had faded away into a low susurration, a hiss of white noise, and then...

"Three. Six. Four. Eight. Eleven. Ten. Nine."

The numbers were issued in a flat monotone, in a vaguely feminine-sounding voice. A seemingly random string of numbers, read in a dispassionate, robotic voice which could be computer-generated for all he knew. Also, though he couldn't tell for sure, he thought the voice issued from the black rectangular box hanging on the front right pole.

A speaker. But why was it playing a random string of numbers? Who was saying them, and why watch and record?

"Twenty-two. Thirty. Eleven. Fifteen. Sixteen. Twelve."

From a second speaker — the front one on the left,

Joey thought — a second monotone voice began reading a string of numbers also. This one sounded distinctly male, in a likewise robotic tone. Impossibly, it spoke its numbers alternating perfectly with the female voice. At first, if Joey concentrated, he was able to differentiate one voice speaking, then the other.

"*Two.*"

"Nineteen."

"*Seven.*"

"Twenty."

The strange part was, though Joey couldn't tell for sure, the female voice never recited a number higher than ten. It kept recycling the numbers 1-10 in a seemingly random order, while the male voice only recited numbers between 11 and 30, also recycling the numbers in no discernable order. He tried to maintain his focus on the alternating numbers to make sure of this, but either the voices had sped up a little and were now overlapping, or he was getting dizzy (he'd had "a little" to drink, after all), because he was having a harder and harder time distinguishing between the voices. They were slowly blending together, the numbers dissolving into a formless mutter.

"*Tres. Ocho. Siete. Uno. Cuatro. Cinco.*"

A third voice - this one in Spanish, was a young girl's voice, also flat and emotionless - joined the cacophony, from one of the back speakers (which one, Joey couldn't tell). Initially, like the first two voices, the Spanish voice recited numbers distinctly from the others, but the longer he listened, the more the little Spanish girl's voice blended into the others, creating an even more jumbled litany of mumblings.

Even so, Joey continued to listen. The longer he listened, the more relaxed he felt. The panicked adrenaline flush he'd felt after the TV screeched had faded. He now felt warm, comfortable, and *high*. That was the only feeling comparable. As if he'd instantly ingested half a bottle of whiskey or smoked several joints in a row. He felt loose and disconnected from everything around him, like he was coated with a thin layer of plastic which insulated him from the world.

He blinked, and realized he'd been staring at the TV for several seconds (minutes?) watching the square space inside the four poles intently, as if waiting for something to happen. It occurred to him, in some distant part of his mind, that the speakers on the poles were projecting the robotic voices and their endless streams of random numbers...

not random

just need to find the pattern

...into the square inside the four poles.

He felt his mouth fall open. Didn't try to close it. A slight trickle of warm saliva ran out of the corner of his mouth, and down his chin. And still he sat, open-mouthed, leaning forward on the sofa, staring into that square, where the robotic voices recited random numbers…

not random

…combined, mingled, and blended together, forming something *new*…

Something in the square shifted.

Maybe it was a trick of the sparse light. A shadow. But on the TV, in that square, something shifted. Light and shadow fluctuated, coiling and writhing in the center of the square, where Joey somehow knew all the voices whispering their numbers were combining, in one place.

"Funfzig. Sechsundfunfzig. Sechzig. Siebzig."

Like the Spanish numbers, he thought this sounded German, but he didn't know any German, so he didn't know what numbers they were. The new voice - of a high-pitched boy, maybe age nine - spoke clearly at first, though just as flat and robotically as the others, and was easy to distinguish from the jumble of voices filling the center of the square inside the four poles. However, this voice also blended with the rest until the only thing Joey could hear were the throbbing, pulsing sounds of commingling voices muttering numbers in many different inflections all at once. Forming a language. An *old* language. A language truer than anything man knew, which spoke to something inside him, making him feel even higher, as if he was drifting free from the world.

Flickers of light and shadow in the square inside the poles pulsed and throbbed as they coiled, growing larger, spreading, filling up the square, *becoming* something. What exactly Joey couldn't tell, because the thing refused to maintain any fixed form his eyes could perceive.

Even so, something was taking shape. Whatever it was called to Joey in a tongue he'd never heard before but somehow understood. In the center of that swirling, twining mass of non-light and non-dark, a great *eye* opened and blinked, but it wasn't a *human* eye, or anything he could conceive of, really. It wasn't like any eye he'd ever seen, and he didn't understand how it was an eye, but it was, and it *looked* at him. Impossible, because he was watching this on a television…

but it didn't feel like that

it felt like he was there

in that room

with the muttering voices and their strange numbers washing over him

…but the great and inhuman eye which wasn't shaped like an eye at all opened and looked at him, out of the TV screen and at him, and into him. Through him. And not only did it see everything, it mirrored what it saw in Joey's eyes and *he* saw everything. He saw the skin of the world peel back to reveal the glistening, pulsing, throbbing innards of the universe sliding and coiling over one another.

Something crossed between a sigh and a moan slipped from Joey's lips. It was cathartic, despairing, and erotic, all at once. He leaned forward, slid off the sofa and onto his knees, and he placed his hands on the flat-screen. The throbbing sounds of all the voices – so many now, so many more than four, speaking in languages no human was ever meant to hear, counting numbers that didn't exist and could never exist – washed over him and into him, filling him up, until he fell away into a cacophonous sea made of inhuman voices muttering unreal numbers.

He plunged all the way to the bottom.

5

onsciousness trickled into Joey's mind slowly. He didn't come awake all at once. His brain registered sensations in gradual flickers of awareness. He felt cold, for instance. Damp. Especially the insides of his thighs, and groin.

Pissed myself, a small voice whispered without shame or embarrassment, distantly factual. *I fucking pissed myself.*

Next, he became aware of stiffness and cramping in his neck. Not blinding pain by any means, but certainly uncomfortable. The way it felt after sleeping in an awkward position, or on the floor. He moved his shoulders experimentally and was rewarded with a fresh bout of not only a pulsing ache in his neck, but also his left shoulder... on which he was lying, apparently. Where he must've fallen when he'd...

Passed out?

The ache was spreading its tendrils slowly up his neck and into his head. A dull monotone began beating behind his still-closed eyes, announcing the arrival of the inevitable hangover headache.

fuck

how much did I drink last night?

Pins and needles spread all through his body, buzzing especially in his left leg. Now that he was waking up and twitching, blood-flow was resuming and his left leg was humming as its nerve endings came alive.

He reached up with his right hand and rubbed his face. He kneaded his temples with his fingertips, as if he could rub his headache away. After several minutes, it did subside slightly. Enough for him to flex his shoulders, brace himself for the inevitable discomfort, and carefully roll over onto his back.

Pain throbbed down his spine, and he gasped. *Shit*, he was fucking stiff. How long had he lain in this awkward-ass position? He must've gotten black-out drunk to have stayed there so long. He stretched his legs tentatively. As it turned out, they didn't hurt as much. The pins and needles sensation in his left leg was slowly fading.

Eyes closed, Joey laid there for several more seconds, carefully stretching his back, shoulders, and legs. The room wasn't spinning, which he took as a positive sign. His body must've processed most of the booze in his system.

Yeah. Got rid of it in your fucking pants.

Just thinking that reminded him of the dampness at his crotch. He caught a whiff of ammonia, too. *Now* he felt disgusted, and ashamed, deciding it was time to get his ass off the ground and into the shower. Hopefully he wouldn't puke when he sat up.

"All right," he muttered, throat faintly scratchy and sore, "fuck it. Get the hell up."

Clenching his hands into fists at his sides, Joey pushed off the floor and eased himself into a sitting position. He swallowed carefully, blinked, and slowly opened his eyes.

Though his head was throbbing slightly worse, his stomach remained relatively still. Hoping his guts would stay that way, Joey sat on his Universal Monsters throw rug in front of his futon, in his piss-damp shorts, rubbing his face, breathing in and out slowly, trying to piece together what the hell happened last night, his crotch feeling damper and colder by the moment.

He groped his still-fuzzy memories for answers and found precious few. He remembered watching *The Stuff* and feeling pleasantly surprised at how culturally relevant it still was. His recollection of *Night Vision* was blurry, however. If his hazy memory served him right, he'd started drinking in earnest halfway through that one. After *Night Vision*, he'd watched…

Joey frowned. He hadn't watched another horror

movie, had he? He'd watched something else. Something odd. A homemade video of some kind, but it hadn't been a movie, or anything gross or too personal. It had been...

Numbers.

Something with numbers. A guy reading numbers into a microphone? No, that didn't sound right. He didn't remember seeing anyone's face. He remembered seeing the back of someone's head, as they sat at a table. Next to an old camcorder on a tripod, recording something.

The four poles. With speakers mounted on them. Speakers issuing those strange voices, of all sorts of different people – adults and children – reading random numbers in different languages. As the voices read the numbers (how many voices had there been?), he'd drifted off until he'd... passed out?

Fallen asleep?

Dozens of voices, all blurring together into one indecipherable mumble, but that mumble had *done* something to him. Made him dizzy, or sleepy, or...

Hypnotized me, he thought. *Fucking numbers hypnotized me.*

Joey snorted. He'd gotten wasted and passed out in the middle of some weird home movie Kretzmer's lawyers had accidently packed into his tote. It certainly wasn't the first time Joey had fallen asleep drunk in the middle of a movie; it definitely wouldn't be the last (though that was a dimly depressing thought).

Of course, he'd never rolled off the sofa or pissed his pants before, but still. First time for everything. Again, the thought this incident was only the *first* of its kind felt distantly troubling.

Even so, another thought registered. *How much of that weird shit did I watch?* He glanced at the VCR and narrowed his eyes. The clock read 4 AM. It had powered off sometime after he'd fallen asleep.

passed out, stinking drunk

or got hypnotized

So had his flatscreen. The tape was ejected, which meant it must've run all the way to the end, then rewound. Of course, whether he'd watched the tape all the way to the end or passed out before that, he had no idea.

At the moment, he didn't care. He'd pissed himself, and more than likely, his Universal Monsters rug. Like a fucking dog. He'd never done that before. He would have to be more careful next time. Have a few beers instead of the hard stuff.

He shook his head and lurched unsteadily to his feet. He waited for just a moment - his thighs and calves still cramping slightly – but after a few seconds passed, he remained upright. His head didn't hurt nearly as much, and he didn't think he was going to puke. Not yet, anyway.

In any case, if he got himself into the shower, washed, and carefully drank a Gatorade, maybe he could grab a few hours of sleep before he met Earl Flannagan at Showbiz Video around nine to load the rest of those VHS tapes and DVDs into Earl's van for transport to the library, where they'd most likely sit on shelves and gather dust until about five or ten years from now, when they were finally discarded, thrown out, or sold off at the library's monthly used books and movies sale. Such an end was ignoble and shameful, but there wasn't anything else to be done. Just like everything else in his life.

Joey shook his head and limped toward the stairs for a shower, telling himself he'd deal with his piss-stained rug tomorrow, also knowing he wouldn't do anything about it at all.

6

Despite setting his alarm for 8 AM sharp, Joey slept until 8:45, blearily opening his eyes to the shrill sound of his smartphone's alarm jangling. He must've dimly heard it going off in his sleep, because he had vague memories of hearing murmuring or whispering, but of course that must've been his phone's alarm, not actual voices. Or at least he told himself that as he stumbled out of bed and around his room, drowsily getting dressed.

After dressing, he stepped into the bathroom and spent a minute or so carelessly combing his hair with his fingers, and then headed for the door and his car. He'd grab something for breakfast from Fast Trac. He was already late, and it wouldn't be long before Earl called to see where he was and if they were still meeting. He briefly thought of calling the librarian clerk and rescheduling, but he forced himself out the door and into his Prius. He wanted this done, so he could at least *attempt* to move on with his life.

Sure enough, just as Joey was turning onto Cranston Street, his smartphone started ringing in its hands-free jack. He glanced at it and saw the call was, indeed, from Earl Flannagan, of Bassler Memorial Library. "Fuck off," Joey whispered as he let the call go to voicemail. "You could stand to be a little more patient, you insufferable tight-ass."

Five minutes later, Joey pulled into the mostly empty parking lot of Showbiz Video. Empty, except for Earl's white Econoline van (who the hell drives one of those things?), which was parked next to Showbiz's front door. Earl was pacing next to his van, smartphone to his ear, most likely leaving Joey a message in his typically clipped, constipated tones. Joey could read Earl's restrained consternation plainly on the librarian clerk's face, and wasn't ashamed at the flash of mean, petty pleasure it gave him.

Well, a voice quipped in his head, *we're a prince today, aren't we?*

Joey shook the voice off, putting it down to lack of sleep, his lingering hangover, and his general mood about Showbiz closing. That, of course, and he'd never liked Earl Flannagan to begin with. He was wound *way* too tight for Joey's tastes.

He pulled up next to Earl's van, parked, and shut the

engine off. Bracing himself for Earl's acerbic and grating personality (the man was about as friendly as a Gila monster), Joey got out of his car, shut the door behind him with a hearty *thunk*, and plastered a jovial grin onto his face as he approached Earl, who'd put his phone away and was now waiting next to his van, arms crossed, face writ with tightly repressed annoyance. He wasn't tapping his foot with impatience, but he might as well have been. "You were supposed to be here by nine."

"Yeah. Sorry about that," Joey said with forced cheer because, of course, he wasn't sorry at all. "Stayed up a little too late last night watching movies, with a little too much whiskey."

Earl didn't comment on Joey's excuse, but his dour expression of disappointment spoke volumes. "I assume all the movies are packed in totes according to genre?"

Joey nodded, somehow managing not to smirk disdainfully. *Of course* he'd separated everything. What did this guy take him for? "I did. Totes are labelled, also."

Earl nodded in turn, his expression doubtful, as if he wasn't sure Joey was being entirely truthful. But then again, that was Earl right down to the ground. He approached the world from a position of wary distrust. "Just so you know, I can't promise we'll keep all of the movies. I have to inventory them first. Make sure they meet the library's standards."

Joey frowned, a flash of irritation pulsing through him. "Ms. Bassler didn't say anything about that. She said I could donate all of them."

Earl pursed his lips, somehow managing to appear prissy and officious at the same time. "Ms. Bassler has an entire library to run. She may have approved your donation, but she certainly doesn't have the time to go through every single movie to judge if they're fit for the library. That's *my* job."

Joey crossed his arms, feeling more annoyed by the moment. Foolish, also. He was acting as if the Showbiz movies were his children. Reacting like a parent being told his kids weren't good enough for a prestigious pre-school. It was silly, he knew. Even so, he couldn't help himself. "How are you determining whether they're 'fit?' You got a handy little rating standard that tells you what's good enough for the library?"

Earl looked a bit taken aback at the vehemence in Joey's tone, which was understandable, because quite frankly, Joey felt a little confused himself. He knew better than anyone that taste was highly subjective. He also knew Earl considered himself just as much of a movie buff as he did. The possibility that he might not want all of Showbiz's movies made perfect sense. It also made perfect sense that Ms. Bassler would delegate the job of donations inventory to Earl. As head librarian, and given her busy schedule in the community, she certainly didn't have an abundance of time to spare.

Even so, Joey had a hard time corralling his anger at Earl. What the *hell* was wrong with him this morning?

Earl quickly composed himself, recovering his officious expression. "It's mostly what our patrons are fond of. For example," he crossed *his* arms, as if mimicking Joey's posture, but he only appeared even more pretentious doing so. "I'm certain our patrons will be interested in your dramas and classics. Documentaries as well. *Maybe* some of the science fiction films, *if* they're classics."

He waved dismissively. "The rest, however? Especially the comedies? I don't think we have any need for those. We *do* have limited shelf space, of course."

Joey cracked his neck, swallowed, and stuffed his hands into his pockets to keep from clenching them into fists. Two competing thoughts waged in his head: *Why am I so pissed over something so stupid?* and *I should kick this motherfucker in the teeth for his disrespect.*

He took a deep breath, troubled by his irrational anger. Yes, Earl Flannagan was a pain in the ass as well as a stuffy, pretentious *dick*. And yes, this was also an unexpected and annoying development. Even so, his anger felt completely disproportionate to the circumstances. He was actually harboring images of curb stomping the motherfucker.

Three. six. four. eight.

Twenty-two. thirty-seven.

Joey's thoughts clouded over. He closed his eyes and rubbed the bridge of his nose between his thumb and forefinger. A dull ache blossomed in his temples.

"You okay?"

Of course, there wasn't even an ounce of sympathy in Earl's voice. Just a snide reference to Joey's drinking, no doubt. His thoughts cleared, however, and the ache in his temples eased. He opened his eyes and said curtly, "I'm fine. So, let me get this straight…"

He trailed off, an icy fist squeezing his guts. His throat closed up so tight he almost couldn't breathe, let alone speak. A chill spread through his body, and he felt flushed with fever and soaked with a cold sweat, all at once.

"What's wrong with you?"

Joey could only gape. Earl's face rippled, its skin melting and pulling back to reveal a gaping maw filled with innumerable teeth, deformed flesh twisting it into a snarl. A serpentine tongue flicked out of the orifice, dripping with a milky-white slime.

"What? What're you looking at?"

The words were understandable English, but they buzzed with an insectile hum, as the *thing's* teeth clicked. More of the skin melted, like running syrup, or soft wax – oozing down the cheeks and neck, revealing a crusted cavity where the nose should be; a cavity filled with the same glistening white mucus which drooled off its tongue. Its eyes glittered, hard black stones, obsidian and shining, and he could *see* his terrified expression reflecting in them...

"*Seriously, Joey... are you okay?*"

The thing – Earl, or whatever the fuck it was – stepped forward, and reached to him... reached a twisted, leathery, four-fingered claw. The fingers were twice as long as they should be, with twice as many joints as they should have. They ended in dagger-like nails of polished black glass, the tips dripping the same whitish fluid.

"Joey!"

Joey blinked, feeling as if he was waking from a deep sleep. Earl took another step closer, now appearing genuinely concerned. He squeezed Joey's shoulder...

When did he grab my shoulder?

...and said, "You're pale white. *Are* you okay?"

Joey's disorientation and crippling fear leaked away, leaving him tired, fatigued, and confused. Something important had happened, but he didn't know what. He had only a vague impression of seeing something awful, and only the faintest wisps of that mind-crippling terror remained.

He looked at Earl. Opened his mouth, closed it, then said slowly, his tongue feeling thick and clumsy, "Yeah. Yeah, I'm fine." He smiled weakly, still feeling out of sorts and off-balance, as a twisted image of Earl looking like *something else* flitted through his mind. "Guess I was up later and had more to drink than I thought."

Earl squeezed his shoulder and once more released it, not looking at all prissy and officious, but all business, if still slightly concerned. "Here's what I'll do. Most likely going to keep the documentaries and period dramas, with maybe a handful of science fiction classics. The comedies we're probably not interested in, but I'll still take them and put them into storage. See how many sell at our next few Saturday used book and movie sales. Do you have any foreign films?"

Joey nodded, almost as taken aback by Earl's sudden shift in attitude as he was by his own unexplained anger. "One tote full, yes."

"Martha Wilkins *loves* foreign films. I'm sure she'll want to check those out of the library, and she'll also recommend them to her friends, so we'll take those, also."

Joey cleared his throat, slowly feeling normal, also feeling faintly ashamed for his absurd rage, and wondering if he'd been reading Earl incorrectly all along. Had the library clerk *really* acted so smugly? Joey no longer felt sure. "What about the rest?" Earl shrugged, his demeanor so nonplussed and relaxed, Joey had to assume he'd completely misread the man. "I'll take them. Will try to sell them at the Saturday sales, also. After about four months, if they don't sell, I'll have to do something else with them. If you've got any preferences…"

Earl paused, suddenly appearing embarrassed, of all things. "I know you wouldn't want them thrown away." Almost completely recovered from whatever the hell had happened, Joey thought quickly. "Handy's Pawn and Thrift. When I had movies no one was renting, the shopkeeper would buy them from me."

Earl nodded. "Good." He gestured at Showbiz Video, which was, of course, Showbiz Video no longer. "Shall we?" Joey hesitated for the briefest of moments. Did the skin on Earl's face ripple slightly? Revealing a leathery, twisted, reptilian face underneath? Did his mouth have too many teeth, and did Earl look at him now with glassy, obsidian eyes? No.

It was Earl Flannagan, Clerk at Bassler Memorial Library, waiting patiently as well as looking at him with a still slightly concerned expression. Joey flickered a smile, nodded, and pulled his store keys (which he had to turn over to Old Man Kretzmer's lawyers Monday) as he turned and walked toward Showbiz Video's front door. He tried not to think too much about how it troubled him to turn his back on Earl Flannagan, for no reason he could put his finger on.

7

It didn't take long to load the totes. They both worked in a business-like silence, only speaking to each other as it related to their task. An hour later, the van loaded, Earl offered Joey his sincere (so far as Joey could tell) thanks, and promised he'd let Joey know if they were taking any movies to Handy's Pawn and Thrift, so long as Joey wouldn't mind visiting the shopkeeper and doing the advance legwork.

Joey agreed readily. It was the least he could do. They shared a brief, perfunctory handshake, then Earl got into his van and drove out of the parking lot.

Joey stood there and watched Earl drive down the street, around the corner, and out of sight. He stood there for several minutes, thinking nothing, feeling nothing, his head filled with a buzzing white noise. In the white noise, he heard…

Voices?

Numbers.

Twelve. fifteen. fifty. six.

He closed his eyes and rubbed his face, feeling tired and worn out. A little nauseous, too. Last night's hijinks were finally catching up to him, probably. On one hand, who could blame him? His one abiding passion was gone. Even though he'd known for years the end was coming, Kretzmer's death had come swiftly, suddenly, and without warning.

In truth, the store's abrupt closing had been far more upsetting than he'd let on to Beth and Tony. Quite frankly, his legs had been cut out from underneath him. Also, as much as he'd tried to tell himself that it all made sound business sense, Joey couldn't help but admit to himself a sense of betrayal that Old Man Kretzmer – Clifton Heights' most reclusive citizen before his death – hadn't found it in his heart to will the store provisions to remain open.

Joey had no claim on Kretzmer's support, and, therefore, no reason to feel betrayed. Kretzmer hadn't known him from Adam. Even so, he still felt betrayed. Let down.

Discarded.

Siete. ocho. uno. cuatro.

Two. eight. eleven.

Even worse?

He couldn't help thinking Beth would feel faintly

ashamed he'd drank so much last night - enough to pass out and piss his pants, for Christ's sake – even if she'd expected it of him anyway.

Eyes still closed, Joey muttered, "What the hell am I going to do now?"

He opened his eyes and dropped his hand limply to his side. He gaped in horror all around him.

Everything was in ruins.

No, not ruins. That didn't do his vision justice. Everything was fucking on *fire* and crumbling to the ground. As if Henry Street had been plunged into the middle of an apocalyptic wasteland, into the depths of hell itself.

Most of the buildings – what *used* to be homes – all along Henry Street were caved in on themselves, ablaze in high, leaping flames. Soot-black smoke boiled into the sky, and whitish-gray ash cascaded down like dirty, polluted snow. Henry Street itself was heaved, buckled, and cracked wide open in multiple places. Smoke poured out of these fissures in great clouds, as if the planet's core was on fire and bleeding.

He turned slowly, feeling strangely disconnected from these hellish sights, his senses muffled. A part of Joey knew he should be skirting close to the edge of madness, but the only emotion he felt was a curious, aching numbness, nothing more.

What had been Showbiz Video was now nothing more than a bombed-out, hollow shell of a building. The roof was collapsed in on itself, and one whole end of the structure was demolished in a cascade of rubble. Like Henry Street, the parking lot – littered with smoldering debris – was heaved and cracked, hissing smoke and soot into the air.

Though he didn't want to, Joey helplessly heeded some deep, inner compulsion, and looked up, *into* the sky.

He saw nothing but unending banks of blood-red clouds. Thick columns of black, billowing smoke rose over the horizon. Through the red clouds and black smoke, he glimpsed things made of shapes neither his eyes nor mind could quite fathom. Clawed and reptilian things they were, and hauntingly familiar. Leathery wings flapping as they flew and dove into each other. Clawing at each other's strange flesh and screaming with cries no human was ever meant to hear.

Joey blinked.

Blinked and saw nothing but the brilliant blue sky of a crisp September morning. A normal, mundane sky, with a scattering of wispy white clouds lit by the rising sun.

He closed his eyes and rubbed them, then opened them again and saw the same. Blue sky. No boiling red clouds, no billowing black smoke, no strange and ancient-looking reptilian monsters tearing each other apart.

When Joey looked down and around him, everything else appeared exactly as it should. Henry Street was also normal, its houses whole and unmarred. Showbiz's parking lot wasn't heaved and cracked. The admittedly empty and forlorn-looking Showbiz Video was whole, also.

An immense weight descended onto Joey's shoulders. He felt bone-weary and more tired than he'd ever felt. Unable to stand in the empty parking lot of his now-empty and dead video store (it might as well be a pile of bombed-out rubble), Joey turned and walked quickly to his car.

He had to get away from this place. He didn't know where to go, but he didn't want to go home.

Not yet. At home, his collection of movies and booze beckoned...

and that weird film... the video with the many numbers

...and Joey figured if he went home now, he'd drink himself into oblivion for the rest of the day. For starters. And then the whole weekend. It was a truth he felt down to his bones.

Maybe if he could find some sort of peace; maybe he *wouldn't* drink himself into another blackout tonight.

Of course, while he was kidding himself, maybe the whole thing was a big mistake. Maybe Mr. Kretzmer's lawyers would call and say they'd made an error and overlooked a slush fund Kretzmer had set aside to keep Showbiz Video open.

Dare to dream, he thought, sleepily, then had to laugh for a moment at his own hubris.

Ha, ha.

Joey got into his car, started it up, and pulled out of the parking lot onto Henry Street, with no clear destination in mind.

8

Boden Hill Trail
Raedeker Park

Though he'd had no intention of it, Joey felt little surprise when he found himself pulling into Raedeker Park's upper parking lot, the closest stop before the Boden Hill Trailhead. A casual, easy-to-walk path which meandered uphill to overlook Ford Hollow and Owen Pond, Boden Hill Trail had been one of he and Beth's favorite trails to walk together. They'd camped on the overlook several times. There was a sad sort of poetry in coming here, now, as it also marked the spot he had lost the thing that had given his life meaning. This was the place he and Beth had both begun and finally ended their relationship.

As Joey walked up the trail, he let his mood drift, only distantly noting the surroundings. Easy to do on Boden

Hill, as the path ran smoothly, with no rocks or ruts to speak of. The air felt cool under the tree-cover, but he didn't mind. He'd never been much for heat, anyway.

The woods sounded oddly quiet. Only a few distant birds called here and there. He hardly noticed, his thoughts occupied with *whatever* the hell he'd experienced in the parking lot outside Showbiz Video. Not only the weird hallucination of that hellish, apocalyptic landscape with things battling in the sky, but also the weird vision of Earl's face melting to reveal something hideous beneath, something with too many teeth and a serpentine tongue…

Joey shook his head and kicked a small rock off the path. It hit a nearby tree with a dull *thunk*. He supposed he shouldn't be surprised. He only drank on the weekends, but ever since Beth called off their engagement five years ago, his weekend movie marathons had turned into drinking marathons more than anything else. Monday through Thursday, he stayed stone-sober. Friday through Sunday, however…

"Never blacked out before," he mumbled as he walked, footfalls thumping the well-worn dirt path. "Never pissed myself before, either."

He shook his head and gazed into the woods, not seeing anything, the thick stands of Adirondack pine and balsam fir trees an indistinguishable brown-green blur. Joey supposed maybe this day was always going to come.

The day when he woke up after a night of binge-drinking to realize he was speeding toward the point of no return, about to career off a cliff and plunge headlong into full-blown alcoholism.

Had he reached that fork in the road where he must choose between seeking out intervention, or saying *fuck it* and drinking himself into an early grave?

A bird called ahead. He glanced up and saw, with a dim sort of surprise, that he'd reached the end of Boden Trail, and was about to step into the overlook. He increased his pace, for some reason eager – anxious? – to reach it. He couldn't imagine why, especially as it was there, around an afternoon campfire, that Beth ended things.

Regardless, he walked quicker. Soon enough, he was stepping out of the woods and into the clearing of Boden Overlook, which loomed above Ford Hollow and Owen Pond. He slowed as he exited the woods and walked to the middle of the clearing where he stopped and took a deep breath.

The air always felt crisper up here, as if it was somehow cleaner and more refreshing. Joey took another deep breath, which served to clear his head some. He looked around the clearing where he and Beth had spent so many nights, sleeping under the stars in the warmer months, snuggled up inside a pup tent in the cooler times.

Everything appeared the same, even though he hadn't

visited this spot since Beth broke off their engagement. The ground was still a sandy mix of Adirondack soil and gravel, as well as old ashes from countless campfires over the years. He saw the charred remains of several, though none of them were fresh. The grass was still the same thin scrub which never grew any higher. Several large stones were arranged in circles around a few of the old campfire sites. Because most of the trees up here were pine, no leaves lay in the clearing, but rather a dusting of brown-red pine needles.

Joey turned full circle, expecting a crippling rush of emotions to overwhelm him in what had once been a special place. He gazed up at the sun, which had climbed through a still bright blue sky. He took another breath and realized he felt *nothing*. Not even a faint, nostalgic ache. He would've thought he'd feel relief at that... but he didn't. He felt absolutely *nothing*.

Joey sighed, stuck his hands into his pockets, and turned to approach the overlook's edge, which dropped off suddenly and sharply toward Ford Hollow below. The hollow wasn't reachable from here. It had its own trail - Ford Hollow Trail, of course – back at the park's entrance. He and Beth hadn't ever hiked that one, however. Nor had they hiked Owen Pond Trail.

Joey gazed out over the pond's blue waters, which sparkled in the sunlight and rippled gently under the light breeze. One thing that didn't make sense and which had been bugging him this whole time, really, in the back of his mind, was blacking out last night. He couldn't make it square in his head. Sure, he'd definitely been drinking and had put away a decent amount of whiskey, but when he'd rushed around his den cleaning up before hurrying off to meet Earl, he'd been surprised at how much Tullamore Dew was left in the bottle on the lampstand. It was still half-full. After waking up on the floor with piss-damp boxers, he would've expected it to be empty, with another started right next to it.

Two. four. one. three. eight.

Ocho. uno. cuatro. dos.

Un. trois.

Thirty. forty-one. fifty-six.

Joey winced as a bright lance of pain stabbed him in the temples. He grunted, closed his eyes, and rubbed the bridge of his nose again. Served him right, he supposed, after how much he'd had to drink last night...

but I really didn't

...but holy fucking *shit* the headaches should be gone by now. He'd been hydrating since he woke up, had choked down four Advil on the way to Showbiz that should've kicked in. He might have to go home and nap for an hour or two if this kept up.

A wave of nausea buffeted him, cramping his guts. He

gasped, bent over, sure he was going to *puke*, for shit's sake, and wouldn't *that* be fantastic? The perfect thing to do up here, where his life turned to shit five years ago.

The nausea faded and his headache passed, but a frigid chill rippled through him, as if the air's temperature had plummeted twenty degrees. Shivering, he straightened, opened his eyes… and stared, a completely different kind of chill spreading gooseflesh along his arms and back.

From his vantage point, he should be looking out over Ford Hollow and Owen Pond. What he saw instead was a blackened stretch of scorched earth, stretching to a vast pit of sludge. Not water, but a thick, black, viscous substance rimmed with yellow scum and full of swirling colors that were… wrong, somehow. As if they were *close* to colors which existed but were also a hair off the normal spectrum.

Behind the pond of black tar wasn't a forest of Adirondack pine, but instead a wasteland of reddish-brown dirt stretching as far as he could see, broken intermittently by black, skeletal, denuded trees.

A great screeching filled the air.

Joey looked up slowly, his gaze drawn irresistibly above him, and saw the skies were once again a molten, swirling red. Pitch black clouds spread across the horizon. As white flakes rained from the sky – flakes of ash which burnt the instant they hit his flesh – dark, amorphous flying shapes roared and collided, clawing each other among the thick black clouds.

Something chittered behind him.

An icy fist clenched his heart. Bands of fear tightened around his chest, making it hard to breathe. Even though he didn't want to, he couldn't help himself. His movements felt achingly slow as he turned toward the sound. He felt sluggish, as if his feet were mired in quicksand. The air thickened, gelling around him as he turned and saw…

An abomination.

It was a cliché and stereotyped expression, but Joey simply couldn't find any other word to describe the *thing* crouching at the edge of the clearing. It scuttled out from behind blasted, charcoal-black and leafless trees, skittering toward him on… legs? Eight or nine or ten, he couldn't tell. Insectile, spider-like, clicking and clacking.

He thought the legs ended in claws which scraped the ground as it scrabbled over rocks and dirt toward him. It moved haltingly in awkward hops and lurches, its distended body, (like something crossed between a small dog and a spider), wobbling unsteadily on its hideous legs, unbalanced, looking as if it couldn't *possibly* be moving so quickly, shouldn't be supported by its spindly legs at all, but still it lurched toward him, hissing from a distinctly snake-like maw lined with an impossible number of teeth dripping a bright green *slime*.

"Oh, fuck," Joey rasped. "Fuck *me*."

The spider-dog-snake-thing hissed again, scrabbled over another pile of rocks, and as soon as its impossibly-clawed legs found purchase on softer ground, it sped toward him, its hissing now high-pitched and angry, its insectile limbs and claws reaching a clacking crescendo. With a lurch which defied all sense of physics and gravity, the thing *leaped* off the ground at him, maw wide, hissing, two long fangs bared, dripping what could only be venom.

Joey reacted instinctively. He screamed and kicked at the thing as hard as he could. He shouted with a strange sort of glee when his boot connected with the thing's bloated body, the impact shivering up his leg all the way to his hip.

The spider-dog-snake-thing flew backwards, its obscene legs flailing, to land on its back at the edge of the clearing.

Joey ran, scrambling for the gap in the blackened trees which might be the opening to Boden Hill Trail. His heart pounding, chest heavy, he expected to hear that thing *hiss* and scuttle after him.

A strange sensation pulsed through him.

Mind spinning, Joey stumbled to a halt. The trees were normal. Nothing but Adirondack pine. He spun wildly and saw Owen Pond as it should be. Ford Hollow was once more full of thick, lush growth. A quick glance upward showed nothing but clear blue sky.

Joey covered his face with his hands. Kneaded his aching temples with his fingertips, and muttered, "What the *fuck?*"

He took two deep breaths, uncovered his face, turned, and strode out of the clearing on trembling legs. He made his way down Boden Hill to his car. He walked in a shaking, shambling lurch, his mind a hissing white noise, and under that sound, he thought he heard…

Numbers.

Two. five. eight.

Zehn. zwanzig. acht.

9

Joey yanked his car door open and fell into the driver's seat. He felt lightheaded, nauseous, and feverish. Beads of sweat peppered his brow, his clothes were damp with perspiration and sticking to his skin, but he also felt chilled at the same time. Classic signs of a virus or bug. That had to be it. He must be getting sick. He'd probably spiked a temperature. How else could he explain the things he'd been seeing all morning?

Joey covered his face with shaking hands. His cheeks felt clammy and cold, but his forehead was warm, and sweat was pouring down his face. He breathed heavily, almost panting, because he'd stumbled blindly down Boden Hill as fast as possible, not daring to look to either side for fear of seeing that black and burnt wasteland again. In fact, several times he thought he *did* see it, from the corners of his eyes. Smoking, charred, skeletal trees and burnt ground under boiling red skies, so he'd plunged down the trail.

His phone rang.

For a moment, Joey sat and stared out his car's front window, mind buzzing with confusion. He felt paralyzed by all the jumbled thoughts and images…

fucking spider-dog-snake-thing

…smashing into each other, while his phone continued ringing, until it finally fell silent, the call probably re-routed to his voicemail.

The silence didn't last long. Almost immediately it started right up again, its warbling sounding terribly shrill in the silence filling his car. The sound pierced the fog over Joey's mind this time, and he fumbled his phone out of his pants pocket. His hands were shaking so badly he almost dropped it, and he had to try three times before he was finally able to thumb the green "answer" icon.

He put the phone to his ear. "H-hello?"

"*Mr. Leonard? I'm glad I caught you. This is Barry Spellman, of O'Hara and Spellman? Mr. Kretzmer's lawyers? I need to talk to you about an urgent matter…*"

"Oh, yeah." Joey drew in a shaky breath. "Those tax papers. For the VHS tapes. I gotta sign them, but I'm not feeling so great. Think I'm coming down with a cold or a fever, or something."

"*Mr. Leonard, it's not about the papers. Those can keep for the moment. No, this is about something else entirely, something far more important…"*

"I'm going to go home and crash for the rest of the weekend. See if I can sleep it off." Joey continued speaking in a rush, the words bubbling out of him. "So, maybe I can come in Monday morning to sign those papers? I'll probably feel better by then. That be okay?"

"Mr. Leonard, you don't understand the urgency of this situation…"

"Thanks Mr. Spellman," Joey said, without listening. "I'll be in first thing Monday morning. Promise."

"Mr. Leonard!"

Joey promptly hung up, switched his phone off, then tossed it into the passenger seat next to him. He started his car up, pulled away from the trailheads and drove out of the parking lot, heading for home, his hands clutching the wheel tightly, cold sweat breaking out on his face anew.

10

The drive back home took forever. At least it felt that way, even though the clock on the car's radio said it only took twenty minutes. The streets stretched out endlessly before him and he clutched the steering wheel with white-knuckled, trembling hands. He stared straight ahead, not daring to glance to either side of the road. If he saw that hellscape again or some other horrible *things*, he didn't think he could take it.

After he finally pulled onto James Street, then turned into his driveway, he shut off the car and sagged back into the seat. He sat there, staring sightlessly out the front window, feeling so tired and rundown, he could close his eyes and fall asleep right then and there. The only reason he didn't was the fear of opening them to once more see a smoldering, red hellscape.

Food, he thought hazily, *I need food. Something to drink, and more Advil. Or maybe some Tylenol. Especially if I have a fever.*

He laid the back of his hand against his forehead, and while it certainly felt damp with sweat, it didn't feel feverish, or even all that warm. If anything, it now felt cold and clammy. Also, he no longer felt dizzy or lightheaded, just tired was all.

Tired.

Hungover.

And maybe he *had* caught a little cold. But the *things* he'd seen. That hideous face behind Earl's skin, the hellscape, that dog-snake-spider creature.

Joey ran a shaking hand through his damp hair, swallowed, and pushed all those thoughts away as he got out of the car and stumbled into his house. Food, water or Gatorade, Advil, Tylenol, in that order. Or maybe Gatorade first. Whatever. He didn't want to think about anything until he'd taken care of the necessities first.

burning red skies

things tearing each other apart amidst black clouds

a fucking dog-spider-snake-thing

Joey closed the front door behind him, deciding that maybe a nip of Irish whiskey might be the first order of business. A little hair of the…

dog-snake-spider-thing

…was always a good idea.

The neck of the Tullamore Dew from last night rattled against the rim of the glass as Joey poured his third two-finger draught. He set the bottle down on the kitchen table, swiped the glass up and tossed back the whiskey with a practiced swallow. It burned a warm, soothing trail down his throat and settled into the already-spreading glow in his belly, which was steadily working to relax him.

Ye gods. Having a few drinks first had certainly been the right call, because that languid calm which came from a bellyful of whiskey was easing along his nerves, soothing him. Maybe he should be worried that he was already floating on a booze-buzz at only 11 AM, but after this morning's experiences, he honestly didn't care. The feverish, hysterical panic that had gripped him on the drive home was slowly loosening its grip.

He'd taken his temperature as soon as he'd gotten inside – a normal 98.7 – and downed four more Advil with a glass of water. Now that he'd taken care of the whiskey, he should get some food inside him.

But when he opened the fridge, he found it half-empty, the only food being unappealing leftovers with questionable shelf-lives. "Pizza again it is," Joey muttered as he shut the fridge door and pulled his phone out of his pocket.

He ordered pizza for dinner at least five or six times a month, sometimes from Chin's Pizza and Wings on

Main Street, sometimes from Pizza Joe's (increasingly from there, actually, because they were cheap, quick, seemingly always open, and the delivery guy didn't do small talk), and sometimes frozen pizzas from Great American Grocery, if he remembered to pick one up on the way home from work. He did buy groceries (after a haphazard fashion), but he often dragged his feet when his supplies ran thin, so it was mostly pizza or other takeout until he finally forced himself to go shopping.

Not for the first time, Joey felt vaguely thankful he enjoyed pizza.

He auto-dialed Pizza Joe's, opting for cheap and no social interaction. Ordering from them was a crap-shoot, though. Sometimes the place was busy for hours and no one ever answered, no matter how many times he called. Sometimes they answered on the first ring, regardless of the time he called. Today it was the latter, for which he was grateful.

"*Pizza Joe's*," came the usual dry, emotionless greeting. "*May I take your order?*"

"Large pepperoni, and an order of garlic knots."

"*That'll be seventeen ninety-five, about twenty minutes.*"

"Great. Storm door cellar entrance around the side of the house, as usual. You know the address?"

"*456 James Street*," the pizza clerk recited robotically.

"That's it. Thanks."

As always, the Pizza Joe's guy said in a flat, toneless voice, "*Thank you for choosing Pizza Joe's,*" and hung up.

Joey stuffed the phone into his pocket, grabbed the bottle of Tullamore Dew and his glass, and left the kitchen to head down to his movie den. The side storm doors entrance led into the den. He always had his takeout delivered there.

Once in his den, he collapsed onto the sofa. He set the Tullamore Dew and his glass on the lampstand next to it, but instead of pouring himself another, he leaned back and closed his eyes. His fatigue from last night, the hallucinations he'd suffered this morning, not to mention the emotionally draining final act of loading all of Showbiz's movies into Earl Flannagan's van, was making itself known, along with the three glasses of whiskey he'd downed. As his breathing slowed and deepened, he felt himself drift into darkness, and he welcomed it, even if he knew it'd only be for another twenty minutes or so.

It would be the last restful sleep he'd ever enjoy.

11

About an hour later, as Joey was about halfway through his pepperoni pizza, his phone trilled Beth's ringtone. He picked the phone up from the arm of the sofa and stared at it as it rang.

Pizza Joe's had been about forty-five minutes late (not unusual for them), which worked out perfectly, as Joey slept soundly the entire time, and felt decently refreshed when he woke up about five minutes before the knock on the basement's storm doors. He and the Pizza Joe's delivery guy, the same guy as always, with a plain face and unremarkable brown hair and brown eyes, exchanged pizza and payment with only a nod, Joey including his usual five-dollar tip. The delivery guy left without a word, which was typical, and Joey retreated to his basement movie den, where he ate pizza and drank several bottles of Gatorade, not wanting to indulge *quite* yet. After his brief but refreshing nap, Joey felt a safe distance from his "troubles" and decided he'd had enough booze to drink for now.

So, he'd spent the next hour eating pizza, hydrating, and watching the classic British television series *Hammer House of Horror* on Shudder. He felt a strange reluctance to watch any more of the VHS movies left to him by Kretzmer, especially not that fucking weird numbers video...

Forty. twenty. ten. thirty.

Siete. ocho. nuevo. seis.

Uno. dos. tres.

...he hadn't even taken the damn thing out of the VCR. Almost as if he didn't even want to *touch* it. Which was stupid, but there it was, regardless.

As he ate and watched campy but still enjoyable British horror, Joey didn't let himself think about his "troubles" from this morning and afternoon. Whenever a stray thought popped up about that hideous visage leering beneath Earl Flannagan's face, or red skies boiling with black clouds and screaming things which tore and clawed at each other, or that awful creature...

fucking-spider-snake-dog-thing

...he repeated the same mantra to himself: *gotta cut back on the booze, gotta cut back on the booze.*

He'd almost managed to make himself believe that, when Beth called. He sat and stared at the phone for several minutes, debating the pros and cons of answering it. Oddly, he felt conflicted. Answering most likely meant admitting he'd had too much to drink last night, which might also lead to telling Beth about that weird movie…

Osiemdziesiąt. dziewięćdziesiąt. trzydzieści.

…and how strange he'd felt this morning, and the things he'd imagined (hallucinated), and he didn't want to do that. And yet, he *did*. He *did* want to tell Beth about it all, because he was afraid of what might happen if he kept it to himself.

The phone fell silent.

A minute later, it started ringing again. Sighing, knowing from experience it was impossible to put Beth off forever, Joey put the phone to his ear and answered. "Hey."

"Hey yourself. How you feeling?"

He paused.

It was on the tip of his tongue to tell her everything. Something held him back, however. Maybe embarrassment. Maybe even a stubborn resentment because she was still checking up on him. No longer together, with no future together – she'd made that clear – and here she was, still checking up on him and acting as if she was concerned for his welfare. Or, maybe, after all this time, she still wanted to control him, even though they weren't together anymore.

That wasn't quite right, and he knew it. Though she'd openly shared her concerns for their future, she'd never once tried to control him, or make him do something he hadn't wanted. Regardless, the thought sparked anger in him as he said curtly, "Sure, I guess. Why?"

Beth must've caught the sharp note in his voice, because she paused before saying, *"Just wondering how you're doing, is all. I know how you get. I mean,"* she added in a rush, almost as if afraid of offending him, *"I know how upset you are about the store closing. Even though you say you're not, I know. I know how you get. Showbiz meant the world to you."*

Even though she was only being the caring Beth he'd always known, Joey felt a surge of anger inside, especially at *I know how you get.* It dug under his skin and rankled him, despite the reality Beth indeed did know. She knew how much he'd been drinking the last few years, and how he tended to self-medicate disappointments with booze. She would also certainly know how Showbiz closing was affecting him. She'd also know how much he was hurting, because she'd be hurting for him.

He should be focusing on that, but instead, he found himself focusing on the rising temperature of that inexplicable *anger* in his guts. "So, you know. So what?"

This definitely caught her off-guard, causing her to stutter. *"I..."* she paused, breathed deep, apparently collecting herself, and said, *"Joey, what's going on? Are you okay? Has something bad happened?"*

Though a part of him (a steadily shrinking part), wanted to tell her everything, even the weirdest things, he instead responded with a harsh question of his own. "Why do you keep calling me?"

"*What do you mean?*"

"Why do you keep calling me? It's over. You ended it. Didn't see a future with a video rental store manager, said my plans were 'short-sighted and too idealistic without any common sense,' so you broke off the engagement. It's over between us. So, why do you keep checking up on me?"

Beth swallowed on the other end of the line. When she spoke, a faint trace of steel vibrated in her tone. "*You know it wasn't that simple.*"

If she thought her tone was going to make him back down, she'd miscalculated, because it only made him angrier. "Honestly? I don't care if it wasn't that simple. We're not together anymore, and you made it clear we had no future. And yet you still fucking call me. Why?"

"*Okay,*" she snapped, "*it's obvious I caught you at a bad time. I'll let you go and call you back later, after you've had a chance to chill out.*"

Chill out.

Chill *out?*

Fuck that.

"I've got a better idea. Don't call me ever again. For *any* reason."

Beth paused for a heartbeat, then said, "*You're not serious.*"

Something in her tone – a sense of smugness, real or

imagined, it didn't matter – propelled Joey to his feet. Suddenly it felt as if his heart was pounding and blood was roaring through his veins. His temples began aching with a dull throb behind his eyes, and his skin felt hot, prickly, and too tight. "I'm serious as *fuck*. We're not together anymore because my job wasn't good enough for you…"

"*It wasn't good enough for* you! You *could've done better!*"

This only spurred him on further and fanned the flames higher inside. "*Whatever.* Bottom line is, we're not together anymore. You have no say in how I live and you *aren't* responsible for me. We're a bit too old to be playing this 'can't we still be friends shit."

"*But I do want to stay friends, Joey. I do.*"

"I *don't.* I want us to be more, and you said we couldn't. But instead of making a clean break so we could fucking move on, you're always calling, prying into my life…"

"*I do not pry!*"

"…wondering how I'm feeling, if I'm okay. You want to know how I'm feeling? Right this moment?" His voice rose at the end and was met with nothing but silence. When she didn't respond, he plunged forward. "I feel shitty. I'm a shit human being who's a waste of space. A loser with dumb dreams anyone could've predicted would fall apart. I've got nothing. No prospects, no future, no one. The only thing I enjoyed doing is gone. I'm fucking drinking too much and seeing things…"

This provoked a startled reaction from Beth. *"Seeing things? What things?"*

"Doesn't matter. What matters is that your calls to 'check on me' and 'see how I'm doing' only make things worse. It tears me up inside every time, because it's a reminder of what's gone and isn't ever coming back. Stop with the half-measures, Beth. Let me fucking *go*."

Silence.

Then a rasping, quiet sob. Some wet snuffles, and then a tense, brittle, *"Fine. Have nice fucking life, Joey."*

The call ended.

Joey stood there, stunned, for several minutes. A tangle of conflicting emotions knotted up his guts. He was furious, because as always, Beth had gotten in the last word. He was also panicking, realizing too late what a raging asshole he'd been, also knowing he said things he'd never meant to (or so he frantically reassured himself), things which couldn't be taken back. He was mourning, because even though he and Beth had called it quits five years ago, their relationship had finally died, right now, with the utterance of a few harsh words.

At the same time, he was furious, simply because he'd let himself go. The control he'd felt so proud of had evaporated in an instant, leaving him an exposed, raw, vibrating nerve. He wasn't even sure *who* he was actually angry at. Beth, himself, or fucking Old Man Kretzmer, for letting Showbiz Video and his future die a pitiful, ignoble death.

Joey didn't realize he'd been standing there in the middle of his movie den, motionless, staring at nothing, until his phone beeped, reminding him the call had ended. He took the phone away from his ear and tossed it carelessly behind him onto the sofa. He grabbed the bottle of Tullamore Dew off the lampstand, twisted the cap off, and tossed it somewhere behind him. He put the bottle to his lips and upended it, taking a healthy slug before coming up for air.

He sighed and closed his eyes as the whiskey warmed and burned him all the way down to his gut. At the least, that whiskey burn – which was hitting him with belated intensity and causing his eyes to water slightly and his nostrils to flare – was waking him up. It was reminding him he was alive, for fuck's sake. Which was *exactly* what he needed to feel, right the fuck now.

He glanced at the Tullamore Dew, now only three-quarters full, looked at the wall clock, which read 1:13 in the afternoon, then back at the Tullamore Dew.

Normally he didn't day-drink, and normally he reserved Sunday for drying out and recuperating for work on Monday. But there wasn't work Monday. He didn't have anywhere to be at all. He had enough money in the bank and enough tucked away in a 401K that he didn't have to start searching for another income source for at least a month, maybe two. He could spend the next *week* drunk, if he wanted. Hell, the next two weeks.

Fuck it.

He took a smaller sip of the Irish whiskey this time and it didn't burn nearly as much. Of course, that was also probably because the booze was starting to perform its magic. Even so, he set the whiskey on the lampstand next to the futon then turned and headed for the stairs to go pick a few more selections from his liquor cabinet. "If I'm going on a binge," he muttered, "might as well do it in style." He had better things to drink besides Irish whiskey, after all.

12

It was seven in the evening, and Joey Leonard was bombed out of his mind. Three sheets to the wind. No, four. Hell, maybe five sheets. Shit-faced. Absolutely, positively, fucked up. Since going back upstairs to raid his liquor cabinet and coming back down into his movie den with Gentleman Jack, Woodford Reserve, and Knob Creek, Joey had sat down on his sofa, poured himself two fingers of Jack, tossed it back, and began sorting through the tote of VHS tapes from Showbiz Video. He selected five or six, and then – throwing caution to the wind – ejected that weird fucking experimental film, tossed it aside, plugged a tape in without looking at it, and started his movie marathon.

He watched one horror movie after another, sipping whiskey, then bourbon, then back to whiskey, along with polishing off the rest of his pizza. He nursed his drinks carefully, however. He didn't want to pass out tonight. He wanted to go the distance. The least he could do was make it to 2 AM this time.

The funny thing was, despite how loaded he was getting, Joey didn't feel the least bit tired at all. He felt possessed by a weird, manic fervor. The air felt charged with electricity, the colors of his HD flatscreen vivid and glowing, and his mind sped along as he watched one glorious '80s horror flick after another. *Mutant, Children of the Night, Chopping Mall,* and *The Suckling.* During *Chopping Mall,* he pumped his fist and whooped when the mall robots blew Leslie's head clean off her shoulders in an almost comical spray of gristle and gore, and he roared with laughter during *The Suckling,* when nuclear waste mutated an aborted fetus into a hooker-killing monster that was a cheap Pumpkinhead knock-off.

He was having a hell of a time. In fact, he couldn't remember the last time he'd enjoyed his horror movie marathons this much.

The only thing nagging at the back of his mind, in a distant, hazy sort of way, was how he ever could've passed out the night before. So far, he'd downed *twice* as much booze (albeit at a slower pace), and he didn't feel near to passing out. Maybe he'd been extra-tired last night, emotionally wrung out from closing Showbiz for the last time.

Of course, there was that numbers video to consider. Fucking weird shit had put him to sleep, or something.

Or something.

Kretzmer's lawyers had called him a few more times, but Joey ignored them. It was because of them, even if only indirectly, that Showbiz Video had closed. He'd go sign their stupid papers whenever. Served the assholes right.

Fuck them all.

As *The Suckling*'s credits rolled, Joey set his tumbler of Johnnie Walker Black - or was it Knob Creek; he couldn't remember - onto the lampstand next to the futon, and eased himself into a kneeling position on the floor next to the gray tote of Showbiz Video's horror movies. Time to find something *really* obscure. He was getting more than a little fuzzy in the head. Pawing through the tote would be the perfect thing to wake him up.

When he opened the tote, however, a cold ripple of shock pulsed through him, bringing a strange kind of clarity. There, lying on top of the other VHS tapes, was the tape with *Numero Vitae* written on the label in black marker.

The numbers video. He'd taken it out of the VCR at the start of the night and tossed it aside. Hadn't he? How had it gotten back into the tote, lying on top of the other tapes, right there for him to see?

He stared at the tape for several heartbeats.

He breathed in, breathed out.

Then, feeling as if he was somewhere outside his own body and not in control, he felt himself reach for the tape and pick it up, then stand and walk slowly over to the VCR. His hands were not his own as he ejected *The Suckling*, inserted the strange tape, and pressed *play*.

The same blue screen appeared, then quickly dissolved into rippling static. After a minute, the static faded, revealing the featureless bare room with the four poles erected in a square, with speakers hanging on them, facing the inside of the square. Without warning, the voices started up at once.

Not like last time, however, with one voice adding its whispered numerical litany at a time. The voices came in one pulsing rush of sound, innumerable voices murmuring a medley of numbers in indistinguishable languages, some he recognized, others completely foreign, and still others sounding inhuman. The numbers blurred and melded together into one amorphous susurration of throbbing, muttering voices, the sound becoming almost a *physical* presence in the room, squeezing his brain and his thoughts into a bright, shimmering funnel.

On the video, a blur began to form in the space inside the poles. A blur which gathered substance and became a pulsing distortion of static. *Waves* of sound. Though that didn't make much sense, Joey knew he was *seeing* waves of sound coalescing and colliding in the middle of those four poles, and not only waves of sound, but the *numbers* themselves were colliding in random patterns which weren't random at all. Colliding, mingling, and *making* something.

The blurry distortion in the middle of the four poles grew into an amoeba of static, its snowy tentacles lashing as it got bigger, wrapping around the poles, almost as if were trying shake them, trying to break free, but somehow Joey knew it was trapped inside the poles, trapped…

Like he was.

Trapped, and unable to escape.

Slowly, his mind heavy and sluggish with booze, Joey stepped closer to the flatscreen, the mass of mingling voices pounding against his brain, as the *numbers*… oh God, the numbers… came together and grew something between the poles in that room, something that writhed, swelled, and surged.

Joey pressed his palms against the flatscreen. Static tickled and buzzed against his flesh, as a faint energy vibrated through his hands, through his wrists, into his forearms, as the voices of millions of different languages blurred the numbers together and pounded them against his brain. He pressed his palms against the screen harder, and thought it was *impossible* – he was drunk, he was hallucinating because of those voices, he had to be – but the flatscreen *flexed*, bowing inward, yielding to his hands' pressure. As if it wasn't a flatscreen at all, but rather a semi-solid membrane separating him from what was on the other side of the screen.

On the screen or the membrane, the room with the four poles and speakers whispering numbers blurred into a swirling whirlpool. Shades of gray, black, and blue mixed and spun, dissolving into static as he *pushed*, feeling the electric buzz as he watched his hands sink into the screen, which stretched into an ever-thinning rubber skin, or maybe even *flesh*. He pushed his arms up to his elbows and even further as the cool, rubbery, slightly moist texture of this strange membrane spread and parted even further as he clawed his way through...

13

Joey stumbled to a halt and nearly fell flat on his face. He'd transitioned almost instantly from his den into a near total darkness. He froze, hands out in front of him, reaching and grasping nothing in the dark.

The *near* dark.

Because a faint light glimmered behind him. A soft, hazy light which cast the barest of illumination in front of him, throwing ghostly flickers of his shadow on the floor, the fuzzy light reminding him of a...

A television glowing in the dark.

Joey took a deep breath and blinked several times, trying to adjust to the dimly lit room he'd stumbled into. His mind raced, thoughts jumbling and slamming into each other, none of them taking hold, slipping through his mental fingers.

Did I blow a fuse? Power go out? Did I forget to pay

my electric... is it overdue already? No, I paid the electric. Power lines down in town? Transformer blow? What the hell happened? Where the hell am I?

Where the hell...

It hit him like a sledgehammer.

He'd been *facing* the flatscreen. Staring into it. *Pressing* his hands against it. Then, he'd pushed, and stumbled through to... Where?

A ball of icy dread curdled in his guts. His mind roaring with white noise, Joey turned slowly toward the flickering, fuzzy glow behind him.

A television, but *not* a flatscreen. It was one of those older big screen televisions, from before the advent of HDTV. It was covered in dust and grime, and its softly glowing screen – which spilled the ghostly light into the dark space around him – was riddled with hairline cracks. And on the television, he didn't see the four poles with speakers from that experimental film, he saw...

His movie den.

There was the sofa, facing the screen, two lampstands on either side. Behind the sofa, lining the far wall, stood one of his VHS/DVD shelves. It was his movie den, where he'd just been. Where he'd been watching the numbers video.

Two. five. one. three. ten.

Uno. ocho. siete. dos. quince.

Stopět. tři sta dva. pět set šedesát.

Yeeogngm yeeogogng. ehyee. ehye yeeogogng.

Joey stumbled back, dizzy and disoriented, his balance wobbly. He could hear them *all*. Somehow, in his head, he could hear millions of voices in languages known and unknown rhythmically and monotonously repeating number sequences over and over.

Something creaked behind him.

Joey spun awkwardly as a quivering sensation gripped his guts. It felt like the sensation of deep tidal and gravitational forces tugging his insides into an infinite number of different directions at once. What he saw before him filled his mind with an unreasoning fear, and he gaped, his mouth hanging open.

It was a basement area which bore an eerie resemblance to his movie den... but it *wasn't*. Instead of his well-worn but comfortable sofa, he saw an old, sagging couch ripped in several places, spilling out clumps of soggy stuffing. The couch was layered with dust and grime. There weren't any lampstands on either side, and no Universal Monsters throw-rug. There was only a dingy concrete floor littered with gravel, leaves, sticks, pine needles, and a strange, rust-red dust.

A glance at the far wall showed him why. It was caved in, and the collapse had brought that side of the house down with it, leaving a gaping hole in the ceiling, through which streamed pale, sickly moonlight. A faint, misty fog clung to the rubble and the ground, curling along as if alive. It crawled down the crumbled masonry, and pooled on the floor at the far end. It looked like a bomb had been dropped on that part of the house, blowing the whole side of it off.

Something creaked again, this time above him, on the first floor, near the stairs. Though he didn't want to, Joey felt himself moving in that direction. Slowly, haltingly, he felt disconnected from his body, out of control, along for the ride. A great pressure filled his head, swelling behind his eyes as he walked toward the stairs.

At the last moment, he stiffened his thighs and locked his knees, bringing himself to a stumbling halt. He didn't want to look up those stairs, didn't want to see what was making those creaks in the floorboards. He thought if he did see what lurked at the top of the steps, he might start screaming and never stop.

He stood there, clenching his muscles, holding himself still, fighting with all his might against the compulsion to stand at the foot of the stairs and look up into the darkness, and see what was up there.

A muffled, wet-sounding *thump* shook the staircase. Then another, and another. Something slowly descending the stairs. A huge and wet body, lurching downward on inhuman feet toward him.

He didn't quite hear the other sound, at first. It was a

low, buzzing hum. A vibration below his range of hearing. It grew steadily as the heavy footsteps thudded wetly down the steps. A chitinous, clacking sound; thousands of locusts swarming.

A tide of darkness surged down the stairway ahead of the heavy footsteps. It poured out into the basement, spreading everywhere, flowing toward him. At first, Joey thought it was some sort of liquid, but as it came closer, he saw the millions of separate parts – bodies – and their twitching feelers, scuttling legs and shining black carapaces.

Beetles.

Thousands, millions, an uncountable number of beetles, each about as big as his hand, moving as one, surging down the steps and all over the floor and toward him as that thing continued to lumber down the stairs.

The sight of the chittering mass of insects snapped the hold of whatever was trying to force him toward the stairway. Joey spun clumsily and stumbled away from the surging flood of beetles, not sure where he was running because where could he run to? He had a vague notion of going back to the big screen TV and trying to push his way through, back to his movie den, back to his world…

His foot caught the edge of the old couch. He pitched forward and fell face-first. His forehead slammed against cold concrete, and pressure instantaneously swelled behind his eyes with such painful intensity he felt sure his eyeballs would pop like blisters.

He rolled over onto his back, gripped both sides of his head. A white-hot hysteria filled him as a blanket of innumerable insectile legs poured over him. He opened his mouth to scream but couldn't as several beetles scrambled up his chest and his neck and jammed themselves into his mouth, clawing their way down his throat, pincers digging into the inside of his trachea as he choked on their thrashing legs and bristling bodies.

14

Joey didn't know what to make of the sound at first. A distant buzzing-vibration. Something humming and rattling and building. It sounded familiar, however. A sound he recognized but couldn't place. It was the electronic modulation of his own screaming, filtered through a million tiny legs, and then…

bzzt

bzzt

A bright flash of fear slammed his mind so hard Joey spasmed upright with a shout, instinctively brushing his hands down his chest and across his lap, batting at something he thought might be crawling all over him…

thousands of shiny black beetles

scuttling all over him

pincers digging into his flesh

…but his hands touched only his clothes, which were

cold and damp with sweat. He instantly regretted moving so quickly, as pain throbbed to life in his temples, and a wave of nausea clenched his guts.

beetles, jamming into his mouth

Light streaming through the ground-level windows hurt his eyes. Vertigo spun the room, and he broke out into a cold sweat as his guts clenched harder.

beetles

in my mouth

The sour taste of bile rose on the back of his throat. He burped, wondering if he was going to puke, knowing he'd never get to his feet and the bathroom upstairs in time.

Joey grasped the sides of his head and closed his eyes, drew in several deep, slow breaths. He swallowed down the bile, and, miraculously, it stayed there. He didn't move from where he lay on the floor, next to the futon. He kept still, eyes closed, taking deep, measured breaths.

After an indeterminable time, his stomach settled. The sour taste receded from the back of his throat. The throbbing metronome in his temples eased.

"What…" he swallowed, and the phantom memory of beetles clogging his throat made his breath hitch. Eyes still closed, he massaged his eye sockets with the heels of his palms. "What. The fucking. Hell."

Joey removed his hands, breathed once, carefully sat up, and then made it to his feet. He turned and stared at his flat screen television. It was dark, its auto timer obviously having turned it off after…

After you passed out again, a voice whispered in the depths of his brain. *After you put in the numbers video, and then you put your hands on the TV screen and pushed and then…*

And then.

Then *what?*

Joey covered his face with his hands and rubbed his temples with his fingertips. God. How much did he drink last night? More than the previous night? He tried to recall, but felt a cold shiver run down his spine as he realized he remembered even less of Saturday night than he did Friday night. *Shit. I must've really cut loose.*

On the heels of that thought, predictably, came a muted sense of shame. That was why Beth called last night. Not because she was trying to control his life. She'd been worried Joey would do exactly what he had: get blackout drunk because of how shitty he felt now that Showbiz Video was gone. As always, Beth had been right on the money. Joey wasn't sure if that was annoying or comforting.

bzzt

rattle

Joey uncovered his face and glanced at the lampstand next to the futon. He knew what that sound was, now. Rubbing the back of his neck with his left hand (his neck felt stiff and sore; of course it did, after sleeping on the floor), he reached with his right hand and grabbed his phone off the lampstand. He swipe-unlocked it to see who was calling.

Even though he was sure it was his imagination, the number on the phone flashed accusingly at him.

Beth.

"Fuck that," he rasped, throat feeling raw and congested. "I don't need this right now." He tossed the phone onto the sofa. It buzzed three more times, then fell silent. If she'd gone to voice mail, it was probably only one of the many messages she'd already left him.

His gaze caught the digital clock on the wall above the flat screen. It read 12:00.

12:00 noon.

He'd slept until noon. Joey supposed he should feel something about that. Surprise, disgust, maybe even shame. He felt nothing, however, except tired and, oddly, hungry and nauseous all at once.

Also, he needed a shower. That was the extent of his emotional response. Past that, he felt numb and hollowed out, and he continued to feel nothing as he lurched toward the stairs and slowly climbed them toward the bathroom. Even as he noticed the strange rust-red dust covering his feet washed off by the shower's sprays and swirling down the drain.

15

After slowly eating a breakfast (past noon) of scrambled eggs and toast, Joey decided to get out of the house. After two nights of uncharacteristically hard drinking...

keep telling yourself that
maybe you'll believe it

...he suddenly felt claustrophobic, as if there was something which clung to him and made his skin crawl, as if *bugs* squirmed beneath his flesh...

beetles

For some reason he thought about the strange red dust he'd washed off his feet this morning in the shower, and that only made him feel itchier.

What he needed, Joey decided, was fresh air, far away from his house, and, ironically, his beloved movie den. It was no longer a sanctuary, a place he could retreat to when the world didn't make sense. The last two nights, his movie den had turned into a drunken, surreal, and nightmarish prison.

It made him both angry and sad. Regardless, at that moment, the idea of hanging out in his movie den turned his stomach. He might be tempted to start drinking again, or maybe even watch the numbers video again, and if he did...

The idle thought occurred that he should eject the tape and snap it in half, then take the remnants out behind his house, pour gasoline over it, and burn it in the fire-pit; or to drive Clifton Heights' backroads and chuck the tape out the window into the woods, but not only did he not want to touch the tape, he was gripped by the ridiculous notion that even if he did get rid of it, the tape would simply reappear in his movie den's VCR.

That of course made him think of the cursed video cassette from *The Ring* and about a dozen other movies which had copied that concept, and how stupid and cliché it was, but somehow that didn't make him feel better at all.

In any case, he couldn't stay home another minute. As soon as he finished breakfast, he dumped his dishes in the sink with several others (doing dishes regularly had become less of a priority lately), grabbed a light jacket from the hallway closet, and left his house with no firm destination in mind. Initially he toyed with the idea of leaving his phone at home but decided against it.

On a whim, he walked past his car parked in the driveway and turned onto Henry Street, deciding to walk into town. It wouldn't take too long. The air was pleasantly cool, and Joey figured he could use the exercise.

As soon as he hit Main Street, however, and turned onto the sidewalk, he regretted his decision. People teemed in moving batches of crowds, back and forth between Clifton Heights' shops and eateries.

Normally, crowds didn't bother him. Normally, he loved walking Clifton Heights' sidewalks on the weekends he wasn't working (or on the weekends he wasn't hungover, a rarer and rarer occasion recently), visiting shops himself, letting the pleasant banter of people wash over him. He normally enjoyed being around his fellow townsfolk, because over the years he'd become a fixture as the manager of Showbiz Video. If there was one person in Clifton Heights who knew movies *and* loved to talk with people about them - Earl Flanagan didn't count; he didn't enjoy talking with *anyone* - it was Joey Leonard. People had gotten accustomed to stopping him on the sidewalk to ask him about movies and what was new in the store, which one they should rent for the upcoming weekend or that night, or to ask him obscure bits of movie trivia. On a regular day, Joey loved every minute of it.

Today, however, Joey found he could barely meet the gazes of others, could barely *glance* at their faces, even. He kept his eyes down and to the side, because every time he glimpsed even part of someone's face, he saw melted flesh running down ravaged cheeks and empty nose-holes wheezing mucus and slime. Patches of white skull gleamed through mangled facial features and dripping viscera. Hollowed-out eye sockets pulsed with a hellish glowing green light. All of them had become decaying corpses, their skulls grinning death's head grins through blood and black sores.

They were monsters. All of them rotting, shambling things whose pulsing organs showed through strips of shredded flesh, grotesque caricatures of humans.

Like yesterday morning and his horrible vision of Earl Flanagan.

Joey kept his gaze down and clenched his hands into fists at his sides. He forced himself not to hyperventilate, even though his heart pounded in his chest and his breath roared in his ears.

Hallucinating, he repeated to himself over and over as he walked forward, shoulders hunched, gaze down and to the right, trying to look at only feet not faces but even the *feet* were wrong. They were grotesquely deformed skeletal feet shiny with musculature and gore. *I'm only hallucinating, that's all, that's all.*

Joey saw he was approaching the corner of Main Street and Acer Street. Inadvertently he glanced up, and the shock of his relief hit him so hard, he practically stumbled to a halt.

Everyone was normal. The sidewalk of Clifton Heights wasn't filled with shambling monstrosities but your average, every-day folks, going about their Sunday afternoon business. Most didn't even notice him. Those who did spared him a glance or maybe a nod and nothing else before moving on.

Joey breathed in deep and ran a hand through his sweat-damp hair. He panned his gaze across Main Street to the other side, thinking, *It was only a hallucination.*

He saw her coming down the front steps of Bassler Memorial Library, on the other side of Main Street. Beth. Walking with her, talking to her, his expression concerned?

Tony Phelps.

He wasn't jealous. Tony was gay, and even if he hadn't been gay, he simply wasn't the type of guy to sniff after an old friend's ex. However, based on both Tony and Beth's worried expressions, Joey guessed what they were talking about. *Him.* Most likely planning some sort of well-meaning intervention.

The last thing he wanted right now was to bump into either of them. It would be awkward in the extreme. He and Beth acting politely, pretending they *hadn't* gotten into a huge fight last night. Tony would act guilty for being caught talking about Joey with Beth, even though both

Tony and Beth would pretend they *hadn't* been talking about Joey.

Or even worse, he'd start hallucinating them as gore-dripping, skeletal monsters. It was something Joey knew he couldn't handle.

Praying to a God he'd never believed in nor had time for, Joey turned sharply right on his heel and headed down Acer Street's sidewalk. A few steps later, he found himself standing before Handy's Pawn and Thrift. It occurred to him this would be an excellent place to kill time, especially because he'd been planning on coming here eventually to let the shopkeeper know he might be receiving some VHS tapes and DVDs from Earl Flanagan, depending on what the library kept.

Also, somehow, he knew there'd be no hallucinating in the thrift shop. It didn't make sense and he didn't know how he knew that, he just did.

The instant Joey pushed through Handy's door, which rang a tiny bell, announcing his entrance, a strange sensation of calm fell over him. The thrift store always had this effect on him, and the shopkeeper's soothing presence had always proved to be a balm. He'd visited this place often after he and Beth broke up, talking obscure film trivia with the white-haired, robust shopkeeper, who knew as much about movies as he did. As Joey slowly wandered down the store's middle aisle, his gaze drifting over its weirdly diverse collection of odds and ends and this and that, he felt ever more convinced that visiting the thrift store had been a good idea.

"Mr. Leonard! So good to see you. What brings you here on this fine Sunday morning?"

Joey smiled instinctively as the shopkeeper stepped out of the store's backroom and approached the sales counter, seemingly materializing out of nowhere, on command. The man had a way of doing that, showing up almost instantly to serve just as soon as someone entered his store. It was almost as if he'd been waiting for you, and only you. It was a touch eerie, but also strangely comforting, too.

Joey approached the front counter, suddenly feeling lighter in step, as if his proximity to the shopkeeper eased his mind, helping him forget his present troubles. "Mostly out for a walk," Joey said, "but also need to give you a heads up about a possible big donation of movies headed your way."

The shopkeeper tipped his head. "Believe it or not, Earl Flanagan has already called me. Said he'd taken most of the movies from Showbiz and wanted to know if I'd be interested in any he didn't think…" he paused, then said with finger-quotes, "'were appropriate for the library's collection.'"

The shopkeeper grinned. "Of course, I said I'd be delighted, *especially* if he didn't think they'd be library-appropriate. Makes my shop the perfect place for them."

Joey chuckled. "I figured. Wanted to make sure."

"You're quite welcome." A pause, during which the shopkeeper's smile faded slightly. "Joey, this may be too intrusive on my part, but I've known you a long time, so forgive an old man his nosiness, but are you feeling all right? You're a bit pale." Joey opened his mouth, but for a moment, couldn't speak. What could he possibly say? That he was seeing things? Terrifying hellscapes, and visions of monsters hiding beneath human faces? He also certainly didn't want to tell the shopkeeper he'd spent the whole weekend drinking himself into blackout oblivion.

it wasn't the booze

it was the numbers

And yet, something inside Joey ached for release. He needed to tell somebody something. Even if it wasn't the whole story. Even if it was only a tiny part. Before Showbiz closed, he and Beth still talked. Despite being ex-fiancés, they'd shared their troubles and worries. But since Showbiz's last day, something had locked up inside Joey. Friday, he'd been unable to tell Beth about the absolute emptiness he felt in the wake of Showbiz's closing.

And after he'd spoken so wretchedly to her last night? They wouldn't be sharing their troubles any time soon. Maybe never again, and quite frankly, he wouldn't blame Beth for writing him off completely. The shopkeeper might be the only person he could talk to. At this moment, anyway.

He swallowed and said, "Actually, I haven't slept well the last few nights. Lots of… bad dreams. Honestly, it's left me worn out."

The shopkeeper frowned and folded his arms, appearing concerned. "I'm sorry to hear that. Do you know why? Is it because of the closing?"

Joey chose his next words carefully. "Believe it or not, it's because of something I *watched*, I think. Not a movie, exactly. But it was… unsettling, and I think that's why I haven't been sleeping well."

"Really? What could *you* have watched which would hamper your sleep?" Simple, straightforward, direct. No snappy remarks about the irony of the town's horror buff not sleeping well because of something he watched. Just a direct, honest question. Joey was reminded again of how much he liked the shopkeeper.

Joey took a few minutes to explain the fate of Showbiz's horror movies, and the VHS tape labeled *Numero Vitae*, and what he'd seen on it. He left out, of course, blacking out Friday and pissing his pants, and last night's strange hallucination of pushing through the flat screen into a hellish version of his movie den.

not a hallucination

As he spoke, the shopkeeper's concerned expression

turned intensely curious. After Joey finished, the shopkeeper held up a finger and said, "A moment."

The shopkeeper pulled a smartphone out of his pocket, swipe-unlocked it with his thumb, and started searching for something, presumably on the internet, Joey figured. He felt a moment of surreal disorientation: the shopkeeper had never seemed the type to own a smartphone. Joey had always entertained the image of the kindly older man being a stubborn Luddite set in his ways. Yet here the shopkeeper was, navigating a smartphone as deftly as any teenager. Joey smiled, amused at his own misconception.

"Ah," the shopkeeper said, "there we are." He set the phone down on the sale counter and tapped it. "Did the numbers sound like this?"

Almost instantly, an adult male began speaking from the phone in dull monotone, reciting a string of numbers. Joey nodded, repressing a shiver. "That's it. Or, at the least, something similar."

Something struck him then, the truth in his words. The number string coming from the shopkeeper's phone sounded similar to those on the tape at home… but *not* the same. The longer Joey listened to them, the less anxiety they produced, until he didn't feel anything at all. *Unlike* the voices reciting numbers on *Numero Vitae.*

"Interesting. That video of yours might have something to do with number stations."

Joey frowned, the words meaning little to him. "What are those?"

The shopkeeper shrugged, expression animated, as Joey had seen him whenever the fellow was talking about a bit of weird trivia which interested him. "No one knows for sure precisely *what* number stations are, though there are generally accepted theories. Independent short-wave radio operators first stumbled across them on random frequencies around the thirties and forties. According to recently declassified government documents, several different federal agencies had discovered them many years earlier. They always sounded the same. Male and female voices, young and old, reading strings of seemingly random numbers with no discernable pattern for three or four minutes, before signing off. They never used the same frequency twice, and often spoke in different languages.

"The predominant theory believed number stations were coded transmissions sent by spies across Europe during the World Wars, and then during the Cold War. And, over the years, several governments have admitted to using number stations to transmit classified information. But." The shopkeeper held up a finger, like an excited professor instructing a lecture hall full of enthusiastic students. "The majority of number stations remain a mystery. What the numbers represent. What information they're transmitting, who's broadcasting them, and from where.

Despite generations of shortwave operators committed to identifying them and decoding them."

Joey's throat tightened. "What else could the number stations be?"

"Besides coded transmissions from spies? The theories are numerous, and each one wilder than the last. Aliens among us reporting back to a scout ship cloaked in orbit. Beings from other dimensions gathering intelligence for their inevitable invasion. Pre-recorded transmissions from an ancient, pre-human civilization with coded, hidden locations of technological marvels which will advance human development hundreds of years."

The shopkeeper smiled, clearly delighted by these outlandish theories. "As you can imagine, science fiction stories and movies have utilized the mystery of number stations over and over."

"Do you think they could…"

cause hallucinations

"…impact someone adversely? If someone listened to them long enough?"

"Ah. You're thinking that watching that video impacted your circadian rhythms enough to cause your recent sleepless nights." The shopkeeper appeared thoughtful. "I'm sure it's possible. You'd be surprised how delicate our sleep patterns are and how easy it is to disrupt them, especially with the stress you must be feeling as a result of Showbiz closing."

Would stress make me see monsters? Hellscapes? Alternate versions of this world?

"I'd suggest getting a good night's sleep tonight. Maybe give movies in general a rest for a few days. Especially that tape."

What if I can't?

What if I can't stop watching it?

What happens then?

Aloud, he began saying, "Yeah, that's a good idea." He flickered a weak smile. "You know me; I get in a rut, and I have a hard time…"

His phone buzzed in his front pants pocket. His initial instinct was to ignore it, but for some reason he couldn't. "Excuse me," he muttered as he pulled his phone out and checked who was calling him, fully expecting it to be Beth again, or maybe even Tony, this time.

It flashed "Spellman & O'Hara."

Kretzmer's lawyer.

Joey stared at the flashing number for another heartbeat. He glanced up at the shopkeeper, whose expression had gone curiously blank, and said, "I gotta go. Need to take this."

He turned and walked away from the sales counter without another word or glance. He answered the call, pushed open the store's front door, and said, "Hello?"

16

"*Mr. Leonard, this is Mr. Spellman again. Please don't hang up. This isn't about the paperwork you need to sign, it's about…*"

"…the videotape," Joey finished flatly as he walked away from Handy's, to the corner of Acer and Main. "Numero Vitae."

A heavy pause hung for several seconds, until, "*Yes. You've watched it, haven't you?*"

Joey stopped short of the corner and leaned back against the outside of Handy's Pawn and Thrift. "I have. Why did Kretzmer have that? And how did it get into my tote of horror movies? Did… did Kretzmer want me to have it?"

"*No. Mr. Kretzmer was a … collector, of sorts. He purchased that particular artifact off what it is popularly known as the 'dark web' years ago. He purchased many… oddities over the years. Oddities which could prove harmful to those unaware of their potential. That tape and several other artifacts were to be disposed of after his passing, as per his will."*

"Then how the hell did it end up in my movie tote?"

"When it came time to dispose of those things, one of his tapes was missing. Numero Vitae. *We contacted Earl Flanagan and he didn't find it in the movies he'd taken from Showbiz, so, we knew – or reasoned – it was in your tote."*

Joey couldn't speak for several seconds. All of this was too crazy. Too bizarre. Everything he thought was true about the world – the universe, even – was tilting on its axis. The ground felt unsteady beneath his feet, his thoughts jumbled and incoherent.

"Mr. Leonard? Are you there?"

Joey closed his eyes and leaned his head back. "Yes. I'm just..." he swallowed down a tight throat. "You said he collected other things. Things which could be harmful. What the *hell* was he collecting?"

Mr. Spellman paused long enough for Joey to wonder if their call had been severed, until the lawyer said, *"That doesn't have any bearing on our discussion, Mr. Leonard, and of course, I've strict confidentiality clauses to abide by, even in Mr. Kretzmer's death. Suffice to say those artifacts have been safely disposed of."*

"This is fucking nuts," Joey muttered, not caring at all that he was swearing over the phone to a lawyer. "Why the fuck would anyone collect shit that was dangerous?"

Mr. Spellman sighed. Joey couldn't tell for sure, but he thought that, in his own way, the lawyer sounded weary, and as frustrated and scared (albeit in a restrained way) as Joey felt. "*Mr. Kretzmer wasn't like other people. I say that factually and without malice. He simply didn't have the same priorities or perspectives as most folks. In my opinion? He collected dangerous things because he, for whatever reason, had a difficult time 'feeling alive.' The entire time I knew him, he never interacted well with people. Properties he understood – he owned over half of Clifton Heights' businesses, you know – and strange artifacts he understood. Those things stood in for the relationships he lacked. In my opinion, anyway.*"

"Okay," Joey said, merely because he'd no idea what else to say.

"*In any case, none of that matters. The important thing is, in your case… Have the visions started?*"

That simple question – *have the visions started?* – crashed down on Joey with the full force of a sledgehammer. Up until that moment, he'd been able, if weakly, to tell himself he was hallucinating. He was tired. Overstressed. Drinking too much. Overemotional. All of which making him see things, and dream things. Now, however, he could not.

"Yes," he rasped, "yes, they have. Have… have you watched the tape also? How do I make the visions *stop*?"

"*In point of fact, I haven't watched the tape, or any of Mr.*

Kretzmer's tapes, for that matter. As for making them stop, there isn't any stopping them, Mr. Leonard. These visions are what led to Mr. Kretzmer's... passing."

A sudden revelation struck Joey. From where he didn't know, but it was true, he knew it. Felt it. "He killed himself. Didn't he?"

Another pause, which told Joey all he needed to know. *"I'm not at liberty to say."*

"Fuck. *Fuck!*" The last came out a little louder than Joey intended, and he glanced toward Main Street to see if any of the passersby on the sidewalks heard. People walked along without giving him any notice, however. "How the hell could number stations make you see things? Make you kill yourself?"

"I see you've done some research. The numbers on the tape are not the same kind of number stations. At least, that's what I gathered from Mr. Kretzmer. According to his research, these are number stations no one talks about. Not shortwave enthusiasts, not the government, no one. No one tries to decode these stations anymore, because whatever information they're transmitting... is deadly and not meant to be known by any man. According to Mr. Kretzmer, all the men involved in the making of that video – part of a clandestine project thirty years ago – eventually all passed in the same manner as Mr. Kretzmer."

"God." Joey closed his eyes again and rubbed the bridge of his nose between his forefinger and thumb. "How do I get rid of the thing? So, it... it doesn't hurt anyone else after I've... *passed*."

"*Destroy the tape. Perhaps, if it's no longer in your possession, the visions will stop, or...*"

Mr. Spellman trailed off, but Joey didn't need him to finish. The implication was clear. "What the hell are these numbers doing to me?"

"*Mr. Kretzmer believed the numbers weren't causing him to hallucinate, but rather, they were... opening his awareness to other worlds. Other possibilities. Or creating other worlds? He was never quite clear on this point. In any case, he believed the number sequences weren't random at all, but rather ancient sequences designed to stimulate the pineal gland, allowing the listener to either see other realities, or create their own.*"

Despite his mood, Joey snorted. "The pineal gland? Great. I'm Jeffery Coombs, and my life is now *From Beyond*."

"*Indeed*," Mr. Spellman said briskly, apparently understanding Joey's movie reference. "*Not to pry, Mr. Leonard, but were you under the influence of any substances while you watched the tape?*"

"I was shitfaced both times. Does that count?"

"*Yes. Mr. Kretzmer preferred a high-grade hashish himself, but yes. Anything which lowers the inhibitions makes it easier for the pineal gland to activate, thus allowing the numbers to more easily stimulate it. Again, this is all according to Mr. Kretzmer's research.*"

Joey shook his head, still struggling to understand, or even believe, despite everything he'd experienced, and had now heard. "Open a door. Create a world. What. The. Fuck."

A sigh on the other end, one which sounded regretful, of all things. "*Indeed. I'm sorry, Mr. Leonard. I believe your time is short. Mr. Kretzmer was able to resist the call of the numbers for many, many years, but only because he'd exposed himself to many arcane forces during his lifetime. You, however…*"

"Not so much, huh?"

"*One thing I can tell you is that shortly before the end, Mr. Kretzmer told me he 'wished he'd had the courage to go all the way.' That he'd had the courage to 'give up this world and accept the other one.' It was as if he believed that if he had done that, he would have survived… somehow.*"

Joey frowned. "What the fuck does that mean?"

The lawyer's shrug was evident in his tone. "*I'm sure I have no idea. Either he was so transformed by his experience he no longer thought in strictly human terms, or he was losing his mind.*" A heartbeat, then, "*You'll destroy the tape?*"

"Yes," Joey lied, "yes I will."

He hung up.

He turned off his phone, pushed away from Handy's Pawn and Thrift and turned toward Main Street, his mind full of nothing but white noise.

17

Joey walked home in a drifting, featureless haze. In a sense, it was a blessing. Even though he again saw the faces of passersby shifting and melting into horrific abominations, and occasionally he caught blips from the corners of his eyes of the same blasted, apocalyptic landscape, he no longer felt the terror which had gripped him before. He felt emotionally insulated, as if he'd smoked a shit-ton of weed and couldn't feel anything. It felt like he was coated in plastic and was viewing the world from a distant, numb perspective.

He had no idea what time it was when he finally reached his house on Henry Street, turned and shuffled up the walk. Somewhere along the way, his phone had slipped numbly from his fingers and clattered onto the sidewalk. He'd left it there and kept walking, not at all worried. The sentiment was trite – hell, cliché, expressed in hundreds if not thousands of horror movies and novels, but still true, nonetheless. Where he was headed, he didn't think he'd need a phone anymore.

Once inside his house (odd how he didn't think of it as a home anymore), Joey almost went straight for the movie den, but recalled what Kretzmer's lawyer said about "lowering one's inhibitions." He made a detour to the liquor cabinet, thought, *Fuck it, let's go out in style*, and grabbed his only bottle of Johnnie Walker Blue. At nearly two hundred bucks a bottle, he only allowed himself a dram every few months. He didn't bother with a glass, however, and took the bottle itself. Somehow, he knew he wouldn't be buying another bottle again. Why not finish the whole thing in one go, and go out with a bellyful of the best?

He didn't watch the numbers right away. Instead, he rummaged through the tote of movies, deciding he was going to watch one last horror movie while slowly sipping straight from the bottle of Johnnie Walker. After several minutes' deliberation, he finally settled on *Phantasm II*, starring Reggie Bannister, the inimitable Angus Scrimm, and James Le Gros, the notorious stand-in for A. Michael Baldwin as Mike.

The irony wasn't lost on him. That last Friday night, which now felt like a hundred years ago, when his life still retained some normalcy, he waxed poetic about *Phantasm II* to Tony Phelps as he closed Showbiz for the last time.

Having eaten a spare breakfast and with not much in his stomach as a result, Joey was already feeling the effect of the whisky as he slowly moved to the VCR and popped in the tape. That was fine. He felt loose, drifting, and free. Beth, old man Kretzmer's suicide, his purposeless future, and his potential – inevitable – demise was distant and unimportant. All he cared about, as he numbly made his way back to the futon while *Phantasm II* began, was watching Reggie and Faux-Mike (as Joey always referred to him) hunt down the Tall Man across a blasted countryside. As a last act, it was a good one.

He settled back into the futon. As the opening title sequence rolled, Joey Leonard tipped the bottle back and drank deep from the Johnnie Walker Blue to begin his last horror movie marathon.

18

He'd only meant to watch *Phantasm II*, but after the movie ended, Joey slipped off the futon (half the bottle of Johnnie Walker was gone), feeling as if every bone in his body had turned semi-solid, and knelt before the movie tote. He rummaged around some more and came up with not one but two more movies. *Dolls*, a loveable movie about killer dolls who befriend a little girl played by Carrie Lorraine, and who subsequently kill off her awful father and stepmother. Second, *Black Roses*, a Lloyd Kauffman Troma film about a demonic rock band spreading its influence (aka, black roses), through its music.

Dolls he enjoyed. It was one of those nineties' movies which somehow balanced heartfelt magic and schmaltz with entertaining death scenes of losers who deserved to die. It was the kind of movie, Joey realized, he would've loved to have shown to his son or daughter when they were old enough, if things had turned out differently between him and Beth.

The thought twisted his guts with remorse and a dull kind of despair. His drinking pace increased to soothe the pain, making the end of *Dolls* fuzzy as his tired and booze-soaked brain had a hard time holding onto the plot. The credits had stopped rolling and the tape popped out of the VCR before he realized he'd stared senselessly at the television during the last twenty minutes of the movie without watching it.

He only made it halfway through *Black Roses*. Not only was his blood-alcohol level reaching a critical mass and he was having a hard time even keeping his eyes open, the demonic rock stars kept hinting at their true evil, devilish faces. That hit a little too close to home for comfort. He clumsily grabbed the remote, clicked "STOP," and somehow managed to lurch to his feet and shuffle to the VCR. He reached down, ejected *Black Roses*, pulled the tape out and tossed it aside. With little to-do, he picked up *Numero Vitae* and popped it into the VCR.

He stepped back and regarded the flat screen as it flashed blue, flashed to a field of flickering static, and then resolved into the hauntingly familiar scene of the featureless room with its four poles with speakers and the man sitting at a table next to a camcorder on a tripod, presumably recording.

The first string of numbers issued forth from one of the speakers. "*Eight. Forty. Sixty. Twenty. Ten.*"

Joey raised the Johnnie Walker to his lips, tipped his head back, and chugged the rest of the whisky. As he did so, a second number sequence began, this time, read by a woman.

"*Five. Eleven. Two. Eight. Four.*"

Joey dropped the now empty whisky bottle. It thumped against his Universal Monsters throw rug with little fanfare, sounding almost anti-climactic. Smoothly – especially considering how much booze he'd downed – Joey stepped closer to the flat screen. He reached out and pressed his hands flat against it. Palms against the screen, he closed his eyes and let the numbers wash over him.

"*Siete.*"

"*Once.*"

"*Seventy-two.*"

Slowly, the voices – of robotic men, women, and strangely sexless children, speaking in an assortment of languages, some of them recognizable, others strange and alien – merged together into a single, throbbing, rhythmic pulse which he felt deep in his gut, all the way to his toes. As the strangely harmonic and unified sound of a thousand voices reading countless strings of numbers in different languages filled him up and moved toward a crescendo, the flat screen felt pliable and semisolid. *Permeable*, like a thin, quivering, fleshy film that he had to push through, if only he was brave enough…

wished he'd had the courage to go all the way

give up this world and accept the other one

Joey Leonard swallowed, focusing on the voices thrumming through him. He flexed his hands and pushed all the way through.

19

A liquid ripping sound, like he was tearing through a thin, wet membrane – as if he was being *born* – filled his ears. A shuddering vibration resonated deep within his guts, and with a jerk, Joey Leonard stumbled *through* and forward several steps.

For an instant, he couldn't breathe. He felt as if an invisible hand was crushing his lungs. He gasped, bent over, hands on knees, black spots forming in his vision. The ground or floor felt unsteady under his feet, and a disconcerting wave of nausea threatened to knock him over. He took several deep breaths and fought against the darkness, pushing back the oblivion of unconsciousness, because somehow he knew if he passed out now, he'd never wake up again.

Maybe that's for the best.

"Give yourself a moment," a deep voice rumbled. "It'll pass." A pause, and then, "For all the good it'll do you."

Though Joey felt certain he'd never heard the voice before, it sounded familiar somehow. A strange sort of calm filled him, and the invisible hand on his lungs eased up. The pounding in his head lessened, and he felt his heart slow. Also, he felt sober, as if the alcohol had been burned out of his system in an instant.

Joey took one more deep breath, gathered his willpower, and straightened, expecting to again see that dismal version of his movie den.

Instead, he found himself standing in the featureless room from the numbers tape. Before him, about ten feet away, stood the four poles with speakers mounted to them. The numbers poured forth, but as they had on the tape, they mingled and blended together into a unified but still disparate pulsing wave of sound which thrummed into the middle of the four poles. And like on the tape...

He could see it.

Where the pulses of sound emitted by the speakers met in the center of the poles, he could *see* what they were doing. Something was forming in the center of the four poles, where the voices repeating number sequences converged into the unified, thrumming pulse. The air rippled and coiled with semi-translucent tendrils and spirals of sound. Sound made nearly physical. Sound made into...

"A doorway," came the rumbling voice from before.

The one he didn't know but somehow recognized. "A doorway to our internal madness."

Joey glanced to his right. There, sitting next to him at a small rectangular table, was the man from the numbers tape, the man he'd only previously seen the back of. Next to him stood a camcorder on a tripod, its lens aimed at the spatial distortion in the middle of the poles. Behind and above the man stood another camcorder on a much higher tripod, aimed slightly downward and at the spatial distortion. It was the perspective of the numbers tape, Joey realized with dim shock.

Joey looked at the man sitting at the table. Stocky, with a bristling crew-cut, a square jaw, and a prominent nose. His face was about as expressive as a slab of granite. As he continued speaking, he never once took his eyes off the throbbing and spiraling waves of sound.

"It's a doorway," the man repeated, "but you've discovered that, haven't you? You've stepped through. If only for a moment."

Joey opened his mouth and tried to speak, but only a harsh squeak came out. He closed his mouth, swallowed, and tried again. "Doorway to... where?"

The man shrugged, his gaze fixed on the whipping and coiling distortion. "I don't know. Another world? *Your* vision of another world, one you created? I have no idea. I never managed to cross all the way over. I didn't have the courage, unfortunately."

Joey's stomach felt cold. "Kretzmer," he breathed. "You're... Archibald Kretzmer."

A slow nod. "I am."

Confusion and dread in equal parts crawled along Joey's brain and clenched his heart. "But... you're dead. You killed yourself. Didn't you?"

Kretzmer shrugged again. "It's hard to remember. The details are... fuzzy. The longer I've been here, the less I recall."

"I... I don't understand. How long have you been here?"

"Not sure. Sometimes, I think I've always been here. Sometimes I think my life in Clifton Heights was a dream, and I never left here in the first place."

Horrifying insight struck Joey. "Your lawyer said you purchased that tape off the dark web. That you bought lots of strange things. But you didn't buy the numbers tape, did you?"

Kretzmer gave Joey a ghoulish grin.

"You were there. You were the one who made it. Doing whatever it was you were doing before coming here... to Clifton Heights."

Kretzmer didn't answer right away. He merely cocked his head as he stared, expression now thoughtful. "It's interesting, isn't it? The longer you hear the numbers without thinking about them, the more they fade into the background, until you don't even notice them at all.

They're still there, of course. The numbers have always been there. Whether anyone heard them or not."

Kretzmer folded large hands on the small table before him. "And, point in fact, I *did* buy the tape off the 'dark web,' but only because I'd destroyed all the other copies thirty years ago. Actually, I thought I'd destroyed them all. Still not sure how one survived, or how it found you. Maybe it wanted to. Whatever that means."

Kretzmer was right. As he talked, the pulsing rhythmic stream of the thousands of voices reciting numbers in uncountable languages faded into the background, but the man's simple mention of them increased their volume, and Joey once again felt their pulse deep in his gut. "What was it, a government experiment or something?" This actually brought a slight grin to Kretzmer's rocky features. "Or something. The government has always known about these numbers. They pre-date the other 'number stations' by eighty years. Guglielmo Marconi, an Italian inventor, activated the first radio in 1895. Before he could send a transmission, he received one: a boy reading a random string of numbers in Latin."

"How… how is that possible?"

Kretzmer cocked his head. "I think the numbers have always been with us. In fact, I think they were here before anything else. Numbers and counting are the universal root of knowledge, after all. They're the root of our existence.

That's where I believe these numbers," he gestured at the whipping, tangling, multicolored tendrils of sound, "come from. The core of all existence.

"You know; most Creation stories begin with a deity saying something along the lines of 'let there be light.' However, some merely say a deity 'spoke creation into existence.' I think that one's correct, and the deity spoke *numbers*, and the numbers created everything."

Joey swallowed with some difficulty, his throat dry and tight. "Why are they making me see such horrible things? Monsters, and… Hell?"

Another laconic shrug. "Who knows? Maybe because you're human and not meant to see the numbers. That's why I'm trapped here, maybe. I performed this experiment thirty years ago. For who or why doesn't matter anymore. All that matters is that I never left this room, and the numbers never left me. That's why I had to have the tape when I stumbled across it on the dark web.

"But I couldn't cross all the way over. Didn't have the courage. So, I'm still here. Probably forever." He paused, then said, "It's not so bad. The numbers become soothing, after a while. They make you forget things."

"But… the monsters. The hellscape? Did you see them?"

"No. Just this room, and that door." He gestured at the spatial distortion. "Nothing more."

"Why am *I* seeing these terrible things? Faces melting off? Monsters fighting in the sky?"

"The numbers are creation. This I believe. Maybe the numbers are creating a world for you. A world you want, deep inside."

Joey gaped, struck dumb by the statement. After several seconds, he sputtered, "Why the *fuck* would I create a world like that?"

Slowly, ponderously, and with great deliberation, Kretzmer turned to look at him again. His face was blank and unreadable, eyes glittering with something Joey thought was madness. Then, he smiled, and it was a horrible thing to see.

"I don't know. You tell me."

The silence stretched for several seconds, filled only with the pulse of voices whispering numbers. Joey desperately tried to look away from Kretzmer's manic eyes, but he couldn't. "I don't understand."

Kretzmer's grin faded as he returned his attention to the doorway, which was growing, now double in size. "Regardless, that's where your answer lies. You must embrace the numbers. Choose them. I didn't, and now I'm stuck here forever. Choose the numbers, Joey. Embrace them."

"How do I do *that?*"

Kretzmer nodded at the disturbance. "There's the door. All you have to do is walk through. Something I couldn't do."

Joey clenched and unclenched his fists. "There's no way back to the real world. Is there?"

"Sure there is. Reject the numbers. Turn your back on them. However, you'll end up here eventually. And then you'll never leave."

Joey stared at Kretzmer's expressionless profile for several minutes, waging a desperate and losing battle inside himself. The thought of going back into his movie den, and eventually committing suicide…

Fuck *that*.

Joey was about to step forward, but stopped as Kretzmer said, "Take this. You might need it."

He turned and saw the man – still staring at the doorway – holding out a .45 pistol. He looked at it questioningly. As if sensing the gaze, Kretzmer said, "I brought it with me in case I needed it when I crossed over. I couldn't cross over, of course, so now it sits here. Might as well get some use out of it."

Joey stared at the handgun for a long moment, then reached out and took it from Kretzmer. Without another word, he strode stiff-legged past Kretzmer and toward the disturbance, toward the doorway.

He tried to make himself simply walk into the four poles and through the disturbance, but he stumbled to a halt, coming up short. He stood entranced by the throbbing waves of sound up close. This near, he could see it wasn't merely translucent, but filled with innumerable threads of light which coiled and twined together. The pulsing rhythm of thousands of voices in thousands of languages reciting numbers washed over him, pulsing along every nerve ending, throbbing deep inside.

Deep in the core of the spatial disturbance, a pulse of light – what color he couldn't tell, because it wasn't any one color at all – beat with the rhythmic pulse of the voices like a gigantic, thudding heart.

Joey believed that Kretzmer was right. The numbers were of creation. Maybe they were the essence of creation itself and traveling through this doorway would be tantamount to the highest order of blasphemy.

But he couldn't go back.

Not because of Kretzmer's warning. There just wasn't anything for him to return to.

A world without purpose. Without Showbiz Video, without Beth, without meaning. He couldn't go back to empty, drunken movie marathons in a den which would soon become a prison, waking up every morning after drinking himself to oblivion in a puddle of his own piss.

The only way was through.

Joey closed his eyes and stepped through the doorway.

20

Nausea twisted his guts as disorientation pulsed through him. A great pressure squeezed his head, like last time, and tugged at his guts. For a moment he felt two invisible hands trying to tear him in half at the middle. He stumbled forward and downward, but somehow, he kept his feet and didn't fall. He steadied himself, breathed in deep, and opened his eyes.

His movie den. Or rather, the dismal, nightmarish version he'd stumbled into before. A dimly-lit, dank basement filled with moldering debris, covered by that same, strange red dust. Empty, lopsided shelves. No Universal Monsters throw rug, just gritty concrete coated by that red dust. The same ragged, sagging, and torn couch spilling its sodden innards everywhere. It appeared the same as before, except...

It was darker this time. No soft glow of a television

behind him. Joey turned slowly, grit crunching beneath his shoes, to where the old big screen television had been before – the window back into his world – except this time, it wasn't a window to anywhere. The old television was dark, its screen spider-webbed with thousands of cracks.

No way back.

Only forward.

Something heavy creaked on the floorboards above, on the first floor. Something *monstrous*, thudding toward the stairs, along with the buzzing, insectile *scuttling* from before, a noise which set his hairs on end and filled his belly with heavy ice.

He *remembered*.

Beetles. Thousands of beetles, crawling over him, pincers digging into his skin, jamming their way in his mouth and down his throat.

Instead of paralyzing him this time, the terror flushed adrenaline through his system, kicking him into motion. He didn't even consider using the .45 Kretzmer had given him. It had six shots at best. He scanned the basement and found that, like his basement, it had a storm door exit leading outside. It was to his left. A short flight of steps led to the storm doors. Even better, they were cracked open.

The stairwell into the basement creaked, as a chitinous rush of many-legged things hissed down the steps. Joey didn't look, fearing that even a glimpse of that horde of beetles might freeze his brain and paralyze him. His legs – rubbery, weak, yet weirdly vibrating with fearful energy – lurched into gear as he stumbled past the sagging old couch. He stumbled up the steps to the storm doors, leading with his shoulder.

The blow jarred him, sending a quick flare of pain through his shoulder and down his back, but the doors – old and riddled with wet-rot – flew wide. He scrambled up the final steps and out into the open, memories of those beetles and their pincers digging into his flesh filling his entire being.

He didn't stop to take in his surroundings or to look at the blasted landscape around him. He ran out onto a heaved and cracked version of Henry Street, and toward where town should be. He didn't dare glance over his shoulder, lest he lose his mind if he saw an endless, bristling blanket of beetles pouring out of the storm doors and across the lawn in pursuit.

21

oey didn't slow down until he'd crossed this world's teetering, rotten version of Black Creek Bridge, which now spanned not water but a river of boiling viscous oil which stank of dead flesh. He came to a sliding halt as he stumbled into Clifton Heights proper, kicking up clouds of that strange red dust, stopping in front of what *should've* been Dooley's Ice Cream and Subs, but was now an abandoned building. His lungs spasmed and his throat itched with the abrasive red dust and he coughed explosively. The dust made him think of asbestos or some other toxic powder.

The red dust is poison, his whirling mind thought, *it's part of what poisoned this... place.*

The air tasted of ash and smoke, and a metallic, chemical sensation slicked the back of his throat. Each breath burned as he stood on the edge of this bastardized version of Clifton Heights, and he gagged on its noxious air.

Why the fuck would I want to create a world like that?

A horrible, edged smile.

I don't know. You tell me.

Joey took one more hitching breath and spat, trying to expel the bitter taste in his mouth, when another memory flashed in his mind, from that last night in Showbiz Video, talking with Tony Phelps.

Phantasm II has to be one of my favorite movies of all time. There's something... simple, about it. Something pure. It's Reggie and Mike, cruising a wasted countryside in the 'Cuda, hunting the Tall Man, and killing monsters. That's it; that's all.

Tony Phelps smiled. Sounds like the perfect world for a horror fan.

A heartbeat passed, then another. "Shit," Joey muttered. "No fucking way."

The numbers are creation.

Maybe they're creating the world you want.

His mind spinning, the .45 heavy in his right hand, Joey straightened, and for the first time, looked fully at the hellscape stretching out before him.

It was Clifton Heights, but everything was coated in the red dust, most of the buildings only half-standing, as if they'd suffered the ravages of a nuclear war. A crumbling Bassler Memorial Library lay across the heaving and cratered street, the ice cream shop to his right and what should be the Radio Shack next to it were burnt and blasted, collapsed in on themselves.

All of them smoldered, sending tendrils of black smoke wafting into the dark and oily sky above where monstrous, shadowy shapes – with no fixed form – roared and attacked each other, claws tearing and teeth rending.

A door slammed open.

A gurgling, phlegmy, rasping sound struck a lance of bright, shining panic through Joey's heart. He looked down from the clawing and tearing shapes in the sky to see an abomination lurching out of the ruined building to his right. It was bipedal, with two arms and legs, but its resemblance to anything human ended there.

Its flesh was rotted and covered with a greenish-black mold amid red and oozing sores. Through the ruined flesh, gleaming bone white flashed. Black veins – thick and throbbing, like hellish nightcrawlers – *crawled* all over its melting body. It reached out claws with obsidian razor tips, and its face (if you could call it that), was split by a maw that was too wide and filled with too many teeth. Its skull was caved in on the top and covered with bits of viscera and gristle.

The thing's maw opened even wider as it let forth a ululating, gurgling scream, and shambled toward him.

Joey froze for a second, limbs locked in terror, belly filled with ice. Then, his mind screamed: *Fuck*! He pointed the .45 at the thing's face and pulled the trigger.

The gun roared, its kick shuddering his arm up to his shoulder. The thing's head exploded into a geyser of wet, fleshy chunks and spongy matter. Hysteria thrummed along Joey's veins, as the thing collapsed into a heap, its ragged neck-stump pumping viscera all over the cracked sidewalk.

A chorus of liquid sounding howls filled the air, coming from all directions. The sidewalks and streets were filling with the things, pouring out of the ruined buildings and hobbling toward him much faster than they should on such ruined legs, arms out-stretched, drooling mouths full of too many teeth, eye sockets blazing a hellish green.

From his left, one of them launched itself at Joey, from the middle of the bombed-out street. He turned, aimed wildly, and pulled the trigger. The gun roared again and blew a gaping hole in the thing's guts, shredding meat everywhere and splattering its entrails to the pavement. As it toppled sideways, Joey caught a glimpse of its knobby spine amid the carnage of its flesh.

Bony claws dug into both his shoulders as one of the things grabbed him from behind, its jagged nails digging into his skin through his shirt. Joey bellowed and spun awkwardly, flinging the .45 up and pulling the trigger. His shot blew away the top of the thing's right temple, spraying dark gray matter everywhere, along with shards of bone. The claws disappeared from his shoulders as the thing toppled backwards.

Joey spun around. They were *all* coming for him. So many hideous, shambling, gore-streaked things with melting flesh which exposed diseased, quivering organs.

This wasn't fucking *Phantasm II*.

He wasn't trolling the wastelands with Mike and Reggie in a tricked-out 'Cuda loaded with cool weapons, hunting monsters. He was about to become *food*, for fuck's sake. His last sensations would be that of his skin being torn off and his organs ripped from his body. This was *Hell*.

Joey bolted out into the street, heading straight into the horde of monsters. The .45 roared three more times, as he blasted away three more shambling things. He blasted away the knee of one, the other its face, and still another he shot in its withered thigh. This opened a gap in the throng that he plunged through, and when he hit the other side of the street, he sprinted away from the horde. He turned wildly and spent another shot, but because he was running it winged uselessly into the air. He turned forward and sprinted for all he was worth.

One of the things burst out of a building to his left, right into his path, turning to face him. Mouth spread wide, drooling black slime which ran down its ruined, cadaverous chest. He slid to a halt, panicked, throwing up the .45, realizing too late maybe he should've used the last shot on himself. Even so, he pulled the trigger.

The thing threw up its hands and screamed, but it screamed "Joey!" in a high-pitched voice he *knew*.

He pulled the trigger all the way back.

The .45 bucked in his hand.

And the bullet smashed into *Beth's* forehead, in the real world. Her head snapped back and blood geysered into the air. Beth crumpled onto her back to a normal sidewalk along Main Street, twitching in an ever-widening pool of blood, eyes wide and sightless, lips moving but issuing nothing but bloody bubbles.

Screams – *human* screams – and shouts filled the air.

Joey stared at Beth uncomprehendingly for several minutes, his mind nothing but the hiss of white noise. And the numbers. The numbers, pulsing in a unified voice of a thousand languages throbbing in his brain, filling him up until there was nothing left.

He sank to his knees in the pool of Beth's spreading blood. As sirens blared in the distance, he stuck the .45 into his mouth and pulled the trigger. A hollow *click* sounded. He pulled the trigger again, and again, and again.

He was still doing that ten minutes later when the police cars sped up to him, tires screeching and sirens blaring, but he didn't hear them. His mind was nothing but roaring white noise and the numbers, and the steady *clicking* of the .45's hammer striking an empty chamber.

CODA

"**I** can't believe it. Can't believe I didn't see the signs, didn't somehow *know*."

Deputy Tony Phelps sagged in the chair across from Sheriff Chris Baker's desk. He covered his face with his hands and rubbed his temples with his fingertips. "I can't believe it," he said again, his voice muffled by his hands.

Sheriff Baker sighed. "Sometimes there aren't any warning signs, Tony. Sometimes things build up so slowly and gradually, gathering pressure, little by little, that nobody notices it, until it explodes."

"I guess." Tony uncovered his face and ran a trembling hand through his hair. "But I saw him Friday night. When he was closing the store for the last time. He seemed fine. Maybe a little depressed, sure. Probably more than he was letting on. And I know he probably spent the weekend drunk. Beth…"

His eyes watered slightly, his breath hitched, and when he continued, his voice sounded rough. "She called me Sunday morning and we met up that afternoon at the library. She told me about the fight they'd had on the phone Saturday night and how nasty he'd been. Said he told her he was seeing things. Still. To do what he did. Run into the street and shoot those people. Killing most of them, killing Beth."

Tony shook his head. "I can't wrap my head around it."

"And you'll never be able to," Chris said softly. "No matter how hard you try. Trust me."

"Yeah." Tony sat forward, looking everywhere but at Chris. "He's still unresponsive?"

"Yep. Completely catatonic. Dr. Jeffers has already processed the admissions paperwork for the Riverdale Institution. He won't stand trial; there's nothing left of him to stand trial."

"Fucking unreal, man. Just so…"

"Tony."

The deputy fell silent, and Sheriff Baker leaned forward. "There's nothing you can do. Go home. Get some sleep. It's terrible and awful and shitty as fuck, but there's nothing else to do but hold onto the ones you love and try to heal. Don't repress your grief, but don't live in it, either. It's the only way."

Tony nodded slowly, patted his thighs, and stood. He turned to leave, but stopped and said, "You know, there's two things that don't make sense about all this, even more than anything else. When they grabbed Joey, he was *covered* in this weird red dust. We don't have any sediment like that around here. Where did it come from?" Sheriff Baker grunted, knowing the second question, but asking it anyway. "And the second?" "Joey hates guns. He doesn't own one. And the gun he had? The .45? It was registered to…"

Sheriff Baker nodded. "I know, Tony. I know."

"But how'd he get it from…"

"Tony."

Tony stopped and looked at Sheriff Chris Baker, a slightly lost expression on his face. "That road is a dead end and one best not traveled. What this town needs now is peace and healing, not probing dead ends that won't do anyone any good."

Tony shook his head, appearing slightly defeated, yet also oddly relieved, as if Sheriff Baker had removed from him a heavy burden.

"Go home, Tony. Take a few days off and get some sleep. Lots of it."

"Sure." Without another word, Tony Phelps thumped the doorframe with his fist as he walked out, and then was gone.

On cue – eerily so – Sheriff Baker's smartphone rang. He picked it up and answered without glancing at the number. "Sheriff Baker."

"Sheriff, this is Mr. Spellman again. Did your men find the item we discussed earlier at Mr. Leonard's home?"

"No. The VCR was empty, and I searched the premises personally, as well as the gray tote you mentioned. Nothing but horror movies. No store-bought VHS tape like you described."

"You're certain."

"As certain as I am of anything, these days."

"Very well. It would be better if the tape was destroyed, but perhaps its disappearance is as good. Best case scenario, it never turns up again. Have a good day, Sheriff. Extend my condolences to those closest to Mr. Leonard."

The line clicked and fell silent.

Sheriff Chris Baker laid his phone on his desk, folded his hands, and sat there for a long time, thinking about Mr. Spellman's words.

Best case scenario, it never turns up again.

That was the problem with a town like Clifton Heights, of course. Lost things always turned up.

Eventually.

THE END

ACKNOWLEDGMENTS

Special thanks to Anika, Maya, and Christian as my first readers, and to Joey Tiderencil and Cecilia Leonard, for letting me borrow your names.

— KL

Kevin Lucia is the eBook and trade paperback editor at Cemetery Dance Publications. His short fiction has been published in many venues, most notably with Neil Gaiman, Clive Barker, David Morell, Peter Straub, Bentley Little, and Robert McCammon. His first novel, *The Horror at Pleasant Brook,* is forthcoming from Crystal Lake Publishing in October 2023.

Printed in Great Britain
by Amazon

24085096R00101